Cecily

ISABELLE HOLLAND

Cecily

a Novel

J. B. Lippincott Company

PHILADELPHIA · NEW YORK

• For Ursula

For Ursula

Cecily

1

"CECILY MATTHEWS."

The child flushed unbecomingly. The rush of color over the rotund cheeks made her look overheated. Her hazel eyes, already fixed on the English mistress, brightened.

"Yes, Miss Marks."

The teacher placed her hand on the open notebook in front of her. She was fair, young and very pretty, but there was a disciplined quality about her near-classic features that made her face seem, in repose, almost austere.

"Cecily, your composition was very good—that is, the content and the way you expressed yourself. It shows," she went on firmly, "what you can do when you try. But the appearance—" With a sudden movement she held the notebook up, facing the classroom. "Really, Cecily, you can write better than this. The handwriting is dreadful, the pages are full of erasures, and your hands can't have been very clean when you wrote it."

At the sight of the sprawling, inky words and the smudged pages the seventeen other girls in the room giggled and glanced at Cecily's sullen, scowling face.

"Stop that." Elizabeth Marks lowered the book quickly. "None of you is good enough to laugh at anyone else."

A touch of regret made her look younger, less remote. She glanced with annoyed apology to the stocky, untidy-looking thirteen-year-old now staring back at her angrily. She started to say something and then simply held out the notebook. "On the composition alone you would have received an A-minus. But I had to lower it to a B because of its messiness."

Cecily got up from the desk and moved towards the front of the form room. Her light blue blouse was pulled almost clear of the navy blue serge skirt, making her short body look even thicker than it was. Her tie had been tugged into a tight knot, and her black lisle stockings lay in wrinkles around her ankles. Surely, the teacher thought, she is the strongest argument yet against a school uniform. But would she look better in anything else? Probably not.

"Hurry up, Cecily. I can't sit here forever holding your book."

Cecily started to move more quickly, half-tripped against the toe of a girl sitting in the tightly packed front row, snatched her book and almost ran back to her desk. Her face was now flaming.

"Apologize to Joan," Miss Marks said evenly.

Cecily stared back for a moment, then glanced grudgingly at the girl over whom she had stumbled. "Sorry," she muttered.

"And Joan," the mistress went on, "apologize to Cecily for pushing your foot out so she couldn't help falling over it."

Joan, an amiable-looking child with red hair and freckles, grinned. "Sorry," she said, in perfect good nature.

Miss Marks smiled slightly. "It's not as though you had little fairy feet."

Joan laughed, displaying two large front teeth with a gap in between, and the rest of the form laughed with her.

"Ann, if you'd just learn the difference between a comma and a full stop, I'd feel my years of teaching had not been in vain. I've made the corrections in red. Write out the whole thing again and this time do it right. Otherwise, not bad." She held out the book amid more laughter, and a small, dark girl went forward to pick it up. She smiled at the mistress, who smiled back. An air of mutual liking lay between the young woman and the children. The notebooks were handed back one by one. The teacher's comments were clear, perceptive and often funny. She was good at her job and knew it. The children knew it too. They liked her with the instinctive liking of the young for someone they can't bully. She was a good disciplinarian and they learned from her.

The one exception was Cecily, who sat like an island that would not be absorbed, emanating, as always, Miss Marks thought with iritation, gusts of emotion: injury, outrage, wild spates of giggles, or spasms of embarrassing, uncontrolled affection. Hopeless. The word hovered in the mistress's mind as the bell rang.

"Homework," she said cheerfully, and started giving out the assignment. "Mary, clean the board please. Ann, Cecily, I want your freshly copied compositions on my desk tomorrow morning. And all of you, stop making so much noise. It sounds like a zoo in here." She swept up her books and stood up, a slender, long-limbed young woman in a powder blue pullover and skirt, her blonde hair almost silver in the sunlight streaming from the window. "Good morning," she said cheerfully.

"Good morning, Miss Marks," eighteen voices replied.

She glanced at her watch and hurried down the corridor through the center hallway with its curving staircase and into the right wing. Ten past twelve. She had the next forty-minute period free before lunch. It would give her time to write a letter to Tim. Conscientiously, she searched her mind for work to be done, compositions to be corrected that would take priority over the pleasure of writing to her fiancé. But she had the gift of working quickly and efficiently. Her work was all caught up.

Mercifully remote from the clatter, the common room lay at the far end of the wing. In between stretched the library, sprawled across what had once been three rooms and reconstructed to preserve as much as possible of the paneling and Regency ceilings.

The left wing, with its newer annex tucked discreetly behind, contained the classrooms, laboratory and gym. The central portion housed the headmistress's office and living quarters, the visitors' sitting room, the sanitarium, where victims of measles, whooping cough and chicken pox were isolated, the school dining room (once a ballroom) and the kitchens.

In front rolled a quarter of a mile of green lawn,

smooth as a cricket pitch and dipping gently to the line of oaks, sycamores and elms that in summer hid the brick wall enclosing the immediate school grounds.

Behind, hidden by the thrusting wings of the house, were the games fields, tennis courts and swimming pool. Beside these, in ranked file, were five more houses, three of them unmistakably Victorian, two built only fifteen years before, shortly after the 1918 Armistice, and almost self-consciously neutral in design, as though the builder, faced with blending three eras of architecture, had settled for as little character as possible. In each house lived approximately thirty girls, ranging in age from twelve to eighteen and brooded over by a housemistress. The oldest and nearest of the houses, St. Margaret's, was connected to the main building by a covered passageway. The others, St. Jean's, St. Clare's, St. Mary's and St. Monica's, were separate. Tucked against the wall near the side gate, an expanded cottage, now St. Elizabeth's, held the juniors, aged six to twelve. Those of the staff who weren't housemistresses lived where they could: the more senior members in the second floor bedrooms of the right wing, the others in the gatekeeper's lodge and a nearby former farmhouse.

Originally called St. Hilda's Academy by its militantly Anglican founder, the school was now almost universally known as Langley School, taking its name from the nearby village. To the south and west the country dipped in gentle folds, its Euclidian pattern of cultivated fields softened by thick hedgerows and stretches of woodland. Behind, to the northeast, it billowed steadily up to the

arching swell of downs. Immediately below the school
lay the village of Langley, containing a church, an inn,
a straggle of houses, one or two shops, a railway station
and a bus stop. Through it ran the main road to the market town of Mainbridge, twenty miles away. Between
Langley and Mainbridge lay the boys' school of Graythorne, where Timothy Nichols, Elizabeth's American
fiancé, was completing his year's stint on an exchange
program as senior history master.

Langley School was neither old nor rich, but under a
succession of canny headmistresses it had acquired a reputation for academic toughness and no-nonsense discipline. The present head, Miss Geoffreys, had resisted the
twin blandishments of easy endowments and social glitter
in the gush of new money after the war. "We are not,"
she said tartly to one socially ambitious parent, shopping
around, "a forcing house for would-be debutantes."

"And thank heaven for that," Elizabeth added, when
she repeated the now-legendary story to Tim. "I've seen
some of those schools—sausage factories for the progeny
of the nouveau riche."

"As opposed, I gather," he replied in his flat Carolinian
accent, "to an establishment like Langley for young fe-
males who are—so to speak—to the levée born."

"It's not as snobbish as all that," Elizabeth protested.
"We have a few exalted offspring. But most are middle
class."

"Pretty high middle, I'd say, at those fees."

She looked at him in exasperation. "Well, you're a fine
one to talk. That place you're teaching at is pretty old-

school-tie. I was there last Speech Day and the place was positively crawling with Old Boys in red tabs and foreign-office hats."

He grinned. "I'm just an exchange interloper and my dangerous ideas are tolerated as temporary and therefore harmless. The boy from the colonies."

"And besides," Elizabeth pursued her point doggedly, "we have some girls on scholarships whose parents are, well—"

"Not quite?"

She grinned. "Quite. And while you're so busy calling the kettle black, what about that college, or whatever you call it, in New England that you're going to be teaching at next year? I read the catalogue you lent me and noted the fees. It doesn't sound to me like an establishment for the worthy poor."

He laughed. "As a matter of fact, it was started as just that. However—touché!"

Elizabeth, walking swiftly down the long passageway that ran past the library, remembered the conversation and smiled to herself. She and Tim had had several such exchanges. A Rhodes scholar, he viewed England and the English with an affectionate, though occasionally satiric, eye. Then suddenly, and for no apparent reason, Elizabeth's mind produced a square, familiar image. Cecily Matthews. Now why, she wondered a little crossly, should she think of the wretched girl at this moment? The answer came immediately in the words "not quite." Cecily spoke in an acceptable accent, yet there was something about her. . . .

Elizabeth slowed and her smile gave way to a slight frown. She could almost see her fiancé's ironic smile. He collected such expressions and enjoyed teasing her about them. She even suspected him of writing them down.

"Are you going to write one of those denunciatory novels?" she once asked him.

"I hadn't particularly planned to. I just get a kick out of these euphemisms, so genteel, so damning."

Usually she laughed it off or, deadpan, laid it on thicker. Lately, despite herself, she'd grown defensive. "Sometimes you sound like a—Bolshevik."

"Sometimes I feel like one, especially when I come flat up against one of your shibboleths. Come out with the wrong vowel sound and you're dead. No good job. No swank club."

"That's simply not true. Look at Ramsey MacDonald."

Tim grinned good-naturedly. Their jousts never seemed to ruffle him. "You look at him. How many Ramsey MacDonalds are there in the Foreign Office, the army, the navy, the Church, or wearing one of those lawyer's wigs?"

She took a deep breath. "I know," she said evenly, "that you're dedicated to the proposition that all men are created equal. I'm pretty dim about American history. But aren't you from one of the states that had slavery? Do you think the Negro in your South feels very equal?"

He sighed. "The chink in the armor, and a big one. No, he doesn't. We're going to have to do something about it. So much for self-righteousness."

"At least we don't pretend."

"That must be a great comfort to those with their noses

pressed to the outside looking in." He glanced at her face and smiled. "All right, honey. Pax."

She swallowed and smiled back. "Pax."

Elizabeth had come to a full stop and stood looking out one of the long, graceful windows that gave onto the back. Running the length of the wing was the pupils' garden: flowers to the left, vegetables to the right, all marked off in neat rectangles. Each lot sported a flat wooden stake, like a standard, on which was penciled the name and house of the young gardener. At right angles to the wing, the main body of the house extended back, its classic length marred by the recent graft of a modern kitchen that bulged, like a growth, out of one side, its garish new bricks clashing sharply with those mellowed by more than a century.

"Perhaps some creeper . . . ?" one mistress had suggested, staring in awe and horror at the new addition, erected during the summer holidays.

"I know it's hideous," Miss Geoffreys replied. "But if you'd spent years trying to explain to the board of governors how insensible modern cooks are to the charms of a traditional range from which they're expected to feed more than three hundred people three times a day, you'd find it positively soothing."

Back of that reared St. Margaret's, railway-station red, its gables and graystone Gothic arches looking like a fester of eyebrows. The passageway that linked it to the main building, referred to by the school as the umbilical cord, was also Gothic and vaguely ecclesiastic. St. Mar-

garet's was the first of the additions to be built, and the
governors were surprisingly protective about guarding
the tender young pupils from inclement weather. By the
time the other four houses went up, an examination of
the budget produced a hardier theory: a little wet never
hurt anyone.

Far to the left ran the school wall, veiled in ivy and
creeper and sheltering along its full circle a wide strip of
flower bed, now blazing with the yellow and blue of
daffodils and hyacinths. There would be carpets of them
at home, Elizabeth thought, rimming the lakes and
marching up the hills. Did they grow wild in the New
England spring, she wondered, or would she have to learn
to live without them? The question brought a curious
pang. It had all happened so suddenly.

She had met Tim at the annual pre-Christmas dinner
dance given by the local bigwig who was patron of both
schools. In that momentous evening they had met and
danced and kissed and fallen in love. The next day,
which was end of term, she had left for Westmoreland.
Two weeks after she returned they became engaged.
Characteristically, she was beginning to decide, he shot
the question at her not when they were kissing in the
dark privacy of his car or lingering over drinks in one of
the oaken booths at the Mainbridge Inn but during a
hasty lunch snatched in a garish café, while she was
struggling with a mouth full of fish bones.

She stared at him, then, without thinking, swallowed
and started to choke.

"For God's sake don't swallow those bones," he said, between amusement and alarm. "Here, take this," and handed her a chunk of bread. "No, don't chew it, just swallow. Why must you eat fish? It looks like wet cotton. Well?" he asked, as she finally emerged, red-faced and breathless, from her napkin.

Her heart was soaring, but she said, "You deserve to be turned down for catching me at a moment like that."

"All the other moments I wanted to ask you, I thought I *would* be turned down. But there was something about you with your mouth full and picking out bones that made you look more vulnerable."

She smiled, her eyes on her plate. "Am I that formidable?"

"Not formidable." He leaned back, searching for a word. "A little quelling, maybe." Then he grinned. "Were you ever a head girl at whatever place you went to?"

"As a matter of fact, I was."

"And a good one, I bet. No stray ends. No insubordination."

Her smile grew strained, but she said lightly, "You make me sound like Queen Victoria—not amused."

A sardonic look glinted in his gray eyes. "Little Queen Vickie, reviewing the troops."

She picked at the fish on her plate in silence, as hurt, pique, anger splintered her happy glow.

He stared at the blonde head bent towards him, the pale gold of wheat. Reaching out, he touched the short, unruly tendrils curling in the steamy atmosphere of the café. "You have beautiful hair," he said. And then, as she looked up, "I'm sorry, darling. I mean about teasing you."

Absurdly, she wanted to cry. "It was such an odd thing to say. I mean, after—after . . ."

His hand, square and strong, closed around hers. "The Nichols finesse, crashing through as usual. Marry me, my darling girl, and I'll try to keep my teasing within bounds."

The tears came, hovering in her eyes. She felt his hand around hers and, looking at his mouth and eyes, felt desire tingle through her body. "Oh, Tim, I want to, I want to. Only—"

The pressure of his hand increased. "Only what?"

Through the urgency that was pushing her towards him, she tried to sort out some dimly felt apprehension: small disagreements, an ironic phrase, an occasional fleeting sense of a fundamental difference, gone at a touch or a glance, routed by the sharp tug of attraction. "Sometimes—I have a—a feeling that I'm not really the sort of person you like."

She hoped, she supposed, for denial. He was frowning, his eyes still on her. But they were aloof now, as though he were contemplating not her but something within himself. The vitality that had always poured out of him, bending and dominating her, had withdrawn, leaving—what? Doubt? Decision? Hope?

She started to withdraw her hand. But his fingers tightened and the remoteness left his face. "I love you," he said, "now and always. Do you love me, Elizabeth?"

"Yes." Her breath caught. "Yes, I do."

"And will you marry me?"
"Yes, Tim. Yes, I will."

The electric bell, marking the beginning of the last period, peeled through the building. With a final glance at the daffodils, Elizabeth turned towards the common room, thrust the door open and walked in.

In the five minutes before the second bell and the arrival of Miss Anson, the French mistress, Cecily stared at her open composition book, at the big "B" in red ink and Miss Marks's small, neat writing beside it. Two smudges at the edge of the page had been circled in red, as had several words that looked as though they had been written on blotting paper. Crossings out were not allowed, so she had erased and written over, and the result looked like the furry legs of a spider. She should, of course, have written the composition out in her rough notebook first and then copied it. But she had left it to the last hour of prep last night, and there was no time.

Remembering the young mistress's cool voice as she held the notebook up before the giggling class, Cecily felt her cheeks start to burn and scowled. When Miss Marks had told Ann Rodney to recopy her composition she had smiled, that rare sweet smile that, combined with her youth and extreme good looks, had given her a passionately loyal tribe of followers. Other mistresses and some of the prefects had tribes too. It made life more interesting to have someone to think and talk about. Some of the less popular seniors indulged in what was derisively known as tribe-hunting, bestowing smiles and indulgent conversation on the juniors. But the tactics were obvious, and the cynical juniors played up and then laughed behind their backs. Not Miss Marks, though, a great part of whose charm was her indifference.

The electric bell shrilled through the building. Girls who had been away from their desks shot back, desk lids banged, chatter subsided. Ann Rodney leaned forward towards a girl on the front row. "I say, Jen, you're going to the play, aren't you?"

Jennifer Williams, form prefect, nodded her curly brown head without looking up from her book. "Umm."

"Let's sit together, then."

"All right." She looked over her shoulder and grinned. "Only shut up now, the Ant will be here any sec." Jennifer was supposed to keep the room quiet until the mistress arrived.

Ann grinned back. "Sorry."

Cecily scowled again, then, with elaborate unconcern, opened her French book. The play was a sore subject. Twice a year each form in the Upper School was taken to a play at the Mainbridge Repertory Theatre. The first time there were four seats short, so lots had been drawn and Cecily had lost. This time there were even fewer seats. Because it was a historical play, Miss Marks, who was form mistress as well as teaching English, had given them to the girls with the highest term average in history. Cecily lost out again.

It's not fair, she thought angrily. Apart from the play the whole outing was a hallowed treat: early supper with

Miss Marks, who acted as chaperone, taxis to Langley station, the train to Mainbridge, hot cocoa and thin slices of bread and butter when they returned. Because they got back after lights out, their beds would be turned down and their hot water bottles filled.

Self-pity filled her. Miss Marks would be warm and friendly, stepping down from her pedestal a little, joining in the jokes, laughingly coping with requests to sit beside her. She was much the nicest and prettiest of the mistresses, jolly and full of fun—if she liked you. Cecily's throat tightened. Tears stung her eyes.

"Do you always read French upside down?" The audible whisper, tinged with sarcasm, came from Cynthia Woolfe, at her right. The girl in front giggled. Jennifer turned her head and frowned.

Cecily glared at her book. "Always," she said loudly. "It's less boring."

"If you don't be quiet, Cecily," Jennifer said, "I'll have to report you."

"Jolly clever," Cynthia murmured, *sotto voce*, "reading French upside down. Fuzzy Wuzzy would be thrilled—"

"I didn't start it," Cecily said.

"Perhaps not." Jennifer's square, rather boyish face was stern. "But do you have to bellow?"

There were two or three stray giggles. "Be quiet, all of you," Jennifer said.

Ann threw her eraser in the air and caught it. "The Ant's late. Hurray."

"Probably gluing down her hair."

"It'd take more than glue."

"Do you think it's a wig?"

"That's enough," Jennifer said, but she was grinning.

Cecily, her sense of injury high, stared across the room at her. She liked and envied Jennifer, who was neither pretty nor brainy but who was popular and had the knack of making people respect her. The need to say something, something funny or clever, to attract the form prefect's attention took hold.

"Fuzzy Wuzzy was a bear," Cynthia crooned softly. "Fuzzy Wuzzy had no hair—"

"So Fuzzy Wuzzy wasn't fuzzy, was he?" Cecily caroled in full-voiced triumph, looking at Jennifer.

But Jennifer's eyes were on the door. There was a moment's total silence, then a rather ragged chorus: "Good morning, Miss Anson."

Miss Anson, alias the Ant, alias Fuzzy Wuzzy, stepped on the dais, strode over to the desk, slapped down her books and swung around to face the class. Beneath the kinky black hair which grew straight out of her head like a gollywog's, her face was rigid. "Whose voice was that I heard screeching down the corridor?"

After another short, tense silence, Cecily said, "Mine, Miss Anson."

"Stand up when you speak to me."

Cecily slid out from the desk and stood up. There were red patches on the mistress's face now. No one moved. Remembering Miss Anson's acid tongue, Cecily felt sick. The silence stretched. Outside, the lawn mower whirred. The warble of a thrush nearby came through the open window along with the smell of wet grass. As Miss Anson's pale blue eyes bored into her, Cecily felt herself getting larger. She wished the mistress would say something, however horrible, to break the stillness that was making her dizzy. To get away from the eyes she stared at the woolly black hair. Fuzzy Wuzzy was a bear, she thought—

"How dare you recite that obscene jingle in the schoolroom!" Miss Anson's high-pitched voice came at her like a saw.

Oh, God, Cecily thought, numb with panic. Did she say the words aloud? "I'm sorry, Miss Anson, I didn't—I mean—"

"No doubt you brought it from home."

Cecily reddened. There was something sickening in the venom behind the insult. Her tongue stuck. Words, jumbled together, clogged in her mind. She had a sudden image of her parents—her father, with his aggressive, North-country manner, her mother, nervously overrefined. Shame filled her, followed by guilt at the shame, then anger, sweeping everything else aside. "No, Miss Anson." Her resonant voice reached across the room. "I learned it here."

"You surprise me. Knowing—"

Cynthia Woolfe rose suddenly to her feet. "Sorry, Miss Anson. I started it. Cecily was just—joining in."

A flood of color drowned the patches on the mistress's face. She neither moved nor relaxed. But in that second she looked defeated. Cynthia was not only the brightest in the form and excellent at French, she was in St. Monica's, Miss Anson's house, and the bitter, adder-tongued woman had made clear her liking.

Cecily stared in surprise and gratitude at her unexpected rescuer. The clever, rather simian face was bland, but the expressive dark eyes held contempt.

Miss Anson blinked. The red receded. The black hair quivered around her head like a wiry fan. Cecily, still angry, wanted to giggle. The teacher's glance broke and strayed across the room. "Who is the form prefect?"

Jennifer rose to her feet. "I am, Miss Anson."

"Then perhaps you'll explain why you allowed this outrageous noise to go on after the second bell."

There was a subtle change in the room. The hunter became the hunted. Jennifer's poise didn't falter. "Sorry, Miss Anson."

Ann Rodney shot to her feet. "It wasn't Jenny's fault, Miss Anson. She told us to shut up."

"Without much effect, obviously." The mistress lowered her meager frame into the desk chair. "Perhaps it's time the form elected someone who has more authority." She looked up, encountered eighteen pairs of hostile eyes and diverted the collective enmity elsewhere. "In your honor, Cecily, the form will do the unseen on page one hundred and twenty by Monday. I'll give you your regular homework later. You may sit down. Will you all please turn to the third conjugation in your grammar books." She glanced over her shoulder. "I thought I asked you always to put the date on the board in French." Her eyes flickered towards Cecily. "I suppose you were too busy being entertained. Fiona, please do so at once."

Cecily slid into her desk. Unhappily aware of the angry glances flung at her she stared at the board where Fiona Dalkeith, copper plaits swinging, was inscribing *Le 14 mars, 1934* in her meticulous, perpendicular script. Fuzzy Wuzzy had won.

Later, she glanced warily at Cynthia and under the sound of opening books and riffled pages whispered, "I didn't know she knew everyone called her that, did you?"

"Of course, fathead! Why do you think she was in such a wax?"

Cecily bristled, was about to reply, when caution prevailed. The Ant had quick ears. She bent her head over her grammar and brooded over the teacher's diabolical revenge. Now everyone was against her. Miserably she contemplated the unpalatable fact that if the tactic had been tried on anyone else—Jennifer or Cynthia or Ann, for instance—it would have backfired. Opinion would have rallied to them, not against them. They were popular, she wasn't.

And then there was the play. This would be the second time running she'd miss, and no one cared. The warm, comforting self-pity that filled her receded abruptly before a sense of discomfort. She wished now that in her first burst of outrage she hadn't written to her parents about the matter. For one thing, it was an admission that she wasn't a blazing success. Her father would find some reason to tell her it was her own fault. And her mother— the thought of her mother's enveloping protectiveness increased her uneasiness. Her mother might—

"Cecily, translate the next sentence, using the conditional tense."

Cecily rose slowly to her feet, trying not to show panic. She hadn't been listening. She had no idea what the next sentence was and only the haziest about the conditional tense.

"Well?"

Something in the teacher's voice, a faintly gloating note, routed Cecily's panic. Quickly she looked at the board, scanning the verb endings listed, and picked at random a sentence two-thirds down the page. *"Je serais toute enchantée de vous voir demain."*

There was a short silence. "Cynthia, translate the next sentence using the past imperfect."

"Nicely fielded," drawled Cynthia out of the side of her mouth as she got up.

"Not at all," Cecily murmured, shaky with triumph and relief. Sliding into her desk she groped for the correct offhand note. "More good luck than management, I expect." And nuts to the whole bang lot of you, she mentally added.

The common room was square and full of light from the five windows lining two sides. Its original grace had been lost when one end had been clipped off to form the corridor outside so that the ceiling seemed to soar over the remaining space. But it was still spacious and airy, and the light pouring in from the south and the west, reflecting off the pale green wallpaper, gave it an arborlike quality. The furniture was old and styleless and comfortable. There were two sofas and several armchairs and in the center a large round table covered with a red cloth. Faded chintz curtains hung at the windows, bookshelves rose on either side of a magnificent chimneypiece, and the worn beige carpet bore light patches where stains had been removed. The fire had been lit and the room was pleasantly warm.

"Lovely," Elizabeth murmured, chilly after loitering in the corridor. The school was centrally heated and the classrooms were, if not comfortable, at least endurable. But the single pipes were no match for the drafts sweeping down the hallways.

There were three people in the room: Miss Hinsley, senior mathematics mistress, Miss Finch, who taught history, and Miss Reynolds, the geography mistress. Miss Hinsley was in an armchair on one side of the fireplace, knitting. Miss Reynolds, opposite her, was reading, and Miss Finch was bent over the table working on what looked like a schedule.

Miss Reynolds looked up and smiled. "Hullo."

Elizabeth dropped her books on the table. "Oof!"

"Bad morning?"

"No, not really. But that child, Cecily Matthews—" She left the sentence unfinished and pushed the short, waving hair back off her forehead.

"Maddening, isn't she?" Miss Reynolds said sympathetically.

"Awful. And she's so messy."

"Spoiled rotten," Miss Finch said, without raising her eyes from her schedule.

Miss Hinsley spoke for the first time. "Yes, but in the wrong way."

Elizabeth grinned. "Is there a right way?"

Miss Hinsley glanced up from her knitting and smiled. She was older than the others, a woman around fifty. The distilled wisdom of thirty years of teaching lay in her face.

"No, but some ways are worse than others. Cecily has been fussed over and cosseted. She has less ability to cope than most children of six. On the other hand, there must have been a shortage of something somewhere. She's anything but sure of herself."

"She's opinionated, though—and quite pushy about it," Elizabeth commented.

Miss Finch looked up. She was a thin young woman with skin, hair and eyes of the same tawny color. "But she backs down fast enough if you start asking for chapter and verse."

"Exactly," Miss Hinsley said. "Among all the other things she isn't sure of, she isn't sure of what she thinks."

"Anyway"—Miss Finch glanced at Elizabeth with a rather tight smile—"she seems to bear you doglike devotion."

Elizabeth frowned. She disapproved of the comment, which she thought in poor taste, and resented the seed of truth it contained. The memory of Cecily's eager look when her composition had been praised, and the flushed, sullen expression on her rather unappealing face when the praise had been followed by censure, passed before Elizabeth's mind. For several reasons it made her uncomfortable. "That's ridiculous," she said.

Opening her notebook, she took out some writing paper and started to clear some space on the table. She wanted to let Tim know that all the arrangements for her leaving at the end of the spring term were falling nicely into place. Miss Geoffreys had been sympathetic about her wanting to return to the States with him after Easter and had asked Miss Finch to fill in as form mistress to the Upper Fourth for the summer term, along with her own Lower Fourth. The fact that Miss Finch did not care for the double-duty arrangement probably accounted for the extra edge to her comments these days. But Elizabeth had the lucky faculty of being indifferent to opinion once she had made up her mind. Tim had to be back in American by mid-May to complete work on his doctorate. They wanted to be married from Elizabeth's home before he left, and she wanted to go back with him. Ergo, Miss Finch would have to lump it.

She maneuvered her paper so that no one could look over her shoulder, even accidentally, and began, *Tim darling*—She paused, pen hovering, and regarded the salutation. It looked wonderful, she thought, and smiled a little at her own childishness.

"Dreaming of orange blossoms?"

The smile vanished. Fifteen times a day Elizabeth reproached herself for snobbery about Miss Finch, whose accent bespoke her grammar-school origin. I don't care where she comes from, she reiterated to herself. But does she have to be so vulgar?

"And cabbages and kings," she said agreeably, and

lowered her head over the writing paper, hoping to end the conversation.

"How does your family like the idea of a Yankee son-in-law?"

Elizabeth bit back a wintry riposte. "Tim wouldn't thank you to call him that. He comes from North Carolina."

"Did he tell you about the slaves on the old plantation?"

Elizabeth laid down her pen and took a breath. Miss Hinsley suddenly stood up, thrust her ball of wool over the ends of her knitting needles and shoved the knitting in a bag. "He probably believes in slavery the way you believe in slave labor camps—for all your admiration for the Great Soviet Experiment."

Miss Finch looked sour. Elizabeth grinned and started back to her letter. She would see Tim on Saturday evening, but that was three days off and she wanted him to have her news as soon as possible. Besides, she liked writing to him. She was amazed to find how much pleasure it gave her to put silly, affectionate phrases down on paper. But then she had been totally unprepared for the hot, sweet pleasure it had given her when he first kissed her, and her reaction to the touch of his mouth and hands. Once, when they were parked in his car in one of the myriad lanes nearby, he had stopped making love to her for a few seconds and said, with surprise in his voice, "This really is new to you, isn't it?"

"Yes," she replied, embarrassed, happy, and—for no apparent reason—near tears.

He kissed her again. "I think when I get back to the States I should write an article on the misunderstood hockey captains of Merrie England."

She pushed away from him. "You're always laughing at us. As though English girls were nothing but bluestockings."

He was still teasing her. "I must admit I was a bit frightened of that forthright, brisk exterior. I can't tell you how delighted I am to find it's just camouflage."

"I suppose all American girls fell into your arms."

"No," he said gravely. "It was a great blow when I found there were a few mulish hold-outs." It was impossible to ruffle him.

"Sometimes you make me sound like a prig."

"That's because sometimes you are one. But you're getting over it nicely." Then, at the look on her face, he said gently, "I love you, and at the fear of turning your fair, pretty head, I think you're wonderful."

She was thinking about this, her pen pressed against the end of her nose, when she became aware that everyone in the room had risen. Sliding a book over her letter, she stood up. Miss Geoffreys, the headmistress, had just walked in.

There was something about Miss Geoffreys that would have made everyone, staff as well as girls, stand up, even if it hadn't been a time-honored custom. Partly it was her age—she was past sixty. Partly it was appearance—her height and chiseled, aquiline features were born to carry authority, and she had carried it with extraordinary success for thirty years. But it was an added quality, underlying her particular blend of intelligence, discipline and kindness, that marked her individuality. Elizabeth sometimes found herself disloyally wondering whether it was the politician's knack for sorting out and remembering the problems and idiosyncrasies of some three hundred staff and girls or whether it sprang from an emotional vitality, a genuine, unforced interest. Those who had worked with Miss Geoffreys a short time liked and respected her, with emphasis on respect. Those who had been with her longer looked up to her with something approaching awe: there was an unpredictability about which of her traits would dominate in a given situation. She despised sentimentality, but she could be unexpectedly gentle (even, it sometimes seemed, lax) and just as unexpectedly tough. The pupils worshiped her.

"Good morning," Miss Geoffreys said pleasantly, and smiled. "Miss Finch, how is the cold?"

Miss Finch gave a thin smile in response. "Better, thank you. Almost gone." Her reply, although courteous enough, sounded like someone who was not going to let charm demoralize her.

"Good. Miss Hinsley, I believe you're taking the Upper Fourth to the play Saturday. How many seats could we get this time?"

The slightest glance passed between Elizabeth and Miss Hinsley. The following Saturday was Elizabeth's night on duty, and she was far too conscientious to ask anyone to change with her, even though Saturday was her evening to see Tim. But Miss Hinsley had suggested it, saying that she had missed the play in London and would enjoy catching the road company. Elizabeth, knowing perfectly well that a weakness for romance beat beneath that aging maiden's starched blouse, had accepted gratefully.

"We were only able to buy twelve together, Miss Geoffreys," Miss Hinsley replied. "It was very popular in London and was sold out in Mainbridge almost immediately."

"Well, we're probably lucky to have those." The headmistress turned towards the windows. "I also came to announce that the school board has at long last agreed that the common room should be redecorated. Now I would like you to decide what paper and material you would like and let me know by the end of the week. Since we've caught the board in a mellow mood we might as well do it properly."

She smiled again and moved towards the door.

"Oh, Miss Marks, may I see you for a moment?"

A little puzzled, Elizabeth followed her out the door into the hallway. Moving beside the older woman, she had the sudden impression that Miss Geoffreys's main intention in coming to the common room was to see her.

"Miss Marks." Miss Geoffreys never addressed any staff member by her Christian name. To do so generally would be unthinkable to anyone of her innate formality. To call some by their Christian names and not others would indicate favoritism or, possibly, condescension. "I received a telephone call this morning from Cecily Matthews's mother asking why, for the second time in a row, she had been left out of those going to the form play.

I'm sure there must be a good reason, but I thought I had better know before ringing her back."

Fair-minded as always, Miss Geoffreys was right to ask. Elizabeth felt she had a perfectly just answer. Nevertheless, she was uncomfortable, as though in some way she couldn't imagine there was a wrong involved.

"Well, there are eighteen in the form. Last time we were able to get fifteen seats—apart from the staff seat, of course. So it seemed the fairest thing to draw lots. Cecily just happened to be one of the three not picked. This time, since we could only get twelve seats and it was a historical play—about the younger Pitt—I thought it would be fairest to pick the twelve who had got the best marks in history for the spring term. The other two who didn't go to the first play were among them. Cecily simply wasn't."

"Yes," said Miss Geoffreys slowly. "It seems a little hard when each form goes only about twice a year."

Elizabeth said nothing because an unpleasant doubt was beginning to crawl across her mind. If Cecily had been anyone else, would this have happened? Wouldn't she have chosen eleven others and said Cecily was to go, marks or no marks? Possibly. Even probably. Her well-trained conscience went on relentlessly. If it had been some girl popular among the others, wouldn't they have, of themselves, drawn lots for someone to stay at home in her place? Almost certainly. They could be cruel and indifferent to the few they didn't like. But to the others they had a strong sense of justice. And shouldn't she, as form mistress, have pointed that out? And now the wretched child had written to her mother, who was always ready and eager to complain. How like her.

They were halfway down the hall now. Elizabeth felt humiliated and annoyed. "I'm afraid you're right, Miss Geoffreys. I'll see the form after lunch and explain and put Cecily on the list."

"Since there are only twelve tickets, you'll have to pull someone else out." Miss Geoffreys seldom queried about direct procedure. But the question "how?" was implicit.

Elizabeth frowned. "Since it was on a marks basis, I'll just take the girl on the bottom of the list off and put Cecily on."

"And who is the twelfth?"

Elizabeth's orderly mind produced, almost photographically, the ranked list of girls. "Ann Rodney."

"Yes, I see. A nice child. Do you think that would be wise?"

As clearly as though she were sitting in the form room, Elizabeth saw what she meant. The moment she announced Ann off the list—and why—the others would turn to the well-liked Ann with cries of "bad luck," "sorry, Ann," and other similar comments. Their slangy schoolgirl sympathy would be a calculated brutality to any sensitivity Cecily might have. A hundred plays would not be worth it. If Cecily were as well liked the comments would be the same, but the tone would be different, very different, and she would be congratulated with impartial good nature. As it was—No, it wouldn't do. The young teacher felt a prod of anger at having spoken before she thought. More humbly, she said, "Do you think I should draw a name out of a hat?"

Miss Geoffreys shook her head firmly. "No. Who is the form captain?"

"Jennifer Williams."

"Is she on the list to go?"

"Yes. About eighth. She works hard but math is her subject."

"Then I would get her aside and explain the situation. She'll probably do it by some way of drawing lots. But it will come better from her, and she'll be able to keep the others in hand."

Strong, capable Jennifer, who kept her head and could exert more influence than any teacher on earth. She didn't like Cecily any more than anyone else did. But she would keep her from getting hurt.

Her pride smarting, Elizabeth said, "Yes, of course that's the way to do it. I should have thought of it."

Miss Geoffreys smiled. Too honest to pretend the idea was anything but her own, she managed to give the impression of taking no credit for it. "And now I'll give myself the pleasure of ringing Mrs. Matthews and telling her that it was a mistake and Cecily of course is going."

"Why don't you tell her the truth, Miss Geoffreys?"

They walked a few steps in silence. "I feel a little like Pilate," Miss Geoffreys said dryly. "What is the truth? I'm sure it was an oversight, but was it exactly a fair arrangement?" She turned and fixed her fine eyes, the color of a northern sea, on the younger woman and drove her foil home. "Do you suppose it would have happened to any but this child?"

"No," Elizabeth said. The shambles was now complete.

"Have you ever met her parents?"

Elizabeth shook her head. "No, I was in charge of the junior house at the Christmas concert. What—what are they like?"

"Her mother is a foolish, intense woman with one child whom she has kept on a leading rein and overindulged. She won't allow Cecily enough independence to develop self-confidence. Her father is a self-made man of enormous pride. He doesn't mean to bully Cecily; he simply wants her to do well. But he goes about it the wrong way and, I suspect, drives her in the opposite direction."

"I see." Elizabeth heard her own voice, untouched and cold.

Miss Geoffreys sighed. "This is neither a reform school nor a psychiatric institution. But we must do the best we can."

Unspoken between the two women lay not Elizabeth's tacit admission that she didn't like the child—the headmistress was too realistic to be disturbed by that—but her unpardonable error in showing it.

They were now in the great, high-ceilinged center hall and stopped at the door of Miss Geoffreys's office. The older woman opened the door and Elizabeth had a glimpse of the paneled walls, the deep bookshelves, the fine desk and red carpet. It was not luxurious, but it was

handsome and full of unself-conscious grace, well suited
to the woman who occupied it. The headmistress smiled.
"Come in a minute."

"Thank you, Miss Geoffreys, but I think I'll try to
catch Jennifer before lunch. I can manage a private chat
with her best then." She didn't want to go in. Her pride
was sore and she felt irked and unresponsive to the other
woman's guarded, circuitous attempt to enlist her sympathy. She smiled and withdrew.

SATURDAY was wet. Elizabeth woke early and for a few minutes lay quite still, her eyes shut, her face half buried in the pillow, and thought, tonight I shall see Tim. Then she opened her eyes and the day rushed in.

Standing in her nightdress by the window, she looked at the bare gray sky and the thin drizzle that seemed to hang like a damp curtain. The lawns and bushes looked sodden and the branches of the trees gleamed black and wet. "Damn!" Elizabeth said aloud.

Because the village complement of taxis would be used for the playgoers, she herself would have to slosh through the wet and catch the bus that passed a quarter of a mile from the school. This would get her to the Mainbridge Inn at about twenty minutes to seven, and there, by herself in the pub, she would have to wait for Tim. She could, of course, telephone him at the school to meet her earlier. But she disliked the idea of doing that even more than the idea of waiting. Blast the play, she thought. It had already caused her enough trouble, what with Cecily and Miss Geoffreys and the awkward interview with Jennifer Williams. Her early good spirits somewhat soured, she snatched up her robe and made for the bathroom.

"Dispiriting weather," Miss Hinsley said at breakfast, tacking into her scrambled eggs.

Elizabeth made a face. "It would have to rain today."

"That's right." Miss Finch delicately buttered a morsel of toast. "It's Saturday, isn't it."

Miss Anson's pale eyes fastened on Elizabeth. "It's fearfully hot in summer in America. They have terrible droughts and the grass, I'm told, is quite brown."

"We could do with some of that heat here," Miss Hinsley said. "I've been freezing all morning. Either St. Clare's furnace is having another crisis or Henry forgot to stoke it."

"Really?" Miss Anson's brows rose. "We've been far too hot at St. Monica's. I really don't care for this new-fangled heating. But then I'm afraid I'm rather old-fash-ioned."

Miss Reynolds looked up with a grin. "Newfangled? Rome had central heating."

A fanatic gleam came into Miss Anson's eyes. "And look what happened to it!"

Miss Hinsley, helping herself to raspberry jam, paused, spoon in mid-air, and laughed. A globule of jam fell onto the white tablecloth. "Bother!" She glanced around at the maid who was busy collecting plates from the staff table. "Sorry, Betty. I've made a mess. If Matron says anything tell her it's my fault."

"That," Elizabeth said dryly, "throws an entirely new light on why Rome fell. You should add a postscript to Gibbon." Why is everyone so foul-tempered, she thought, and then added justly, including me. Usually she enjoyed breakfast and didn't mind the inevitable clatter coming from the long tables where the girls were seated. This morning it got on her nerves. She glanced across the room. The staff table, on a shallow dais at the far end of the dining room just in front of the long windows, spanned the width of the room and was at right angles to the other tables. Elizabeth, with her back to the light and an empty seat in front of her, could see easily. Prefects were assigned to the ends of the tables, but the rest of the girls sat according to a system designed to break up houses, forms and cliques. As each girl entered the dining room she took a disc bearing a letter and a number. The letter indicated the table, and the number her seat at it.

Elizabeth's eyes, straying across the room, encountered Cecily, halfway down a table at the right, demolishing a piece of bread and jam. She was doing it neatly enough, cutting her bread into four and applying jam to each piece separately. But she was going at it with single-minded enthusiasm. The girls around her weren't exactly nibbling, Elizabeth thought, but neither did they stoke. Cecily, unquestionably, did. She glanced down at her own half-eaten plate, ashamed of her sudden spasm of irritation. In her four years of teaching she had never had any trouble with her reactions to those she had taught. Obviously she had liked some better than others. But for the first time she was having to struggle with a stubborn, growing dislike. Her mind slid to the head-mistress's implicit reprimand, and her irritation increased. Never before had she been reproved for her treatment of a pupil. She looked back at Cecily, who was helping her-self to another piece of bread.

"She's going to weigh a ton if she doesn't stop stuffing herself," Elizabeth said suddenly.

Miss Hinsley, beside her, glanced up. "Who?" She followed Elizabeth's gaze. "Yes, I'm afraid so. Still, some of it may be puppy fat, and sheer vanity may save the day in a year or so." She paused and then said, "I take it Cecily's going to the play."

So the head had gossiped to Miss Hinsley, Elizabeth thought. Resentment followed surprise. Now the slap was public. "I suppose Miss Geoffreys talked to you about it."

"No, she didn't." Miss Hinsley hesitated and gave a wry smile. "I won't say I didn't know she knew about it, because she always knows about everything. How, I don't know. Pure intuition, I sometimes think. But she certainly didn't say anything to me. She wouldn't. You should know that, Elizabeth. I got it from Jennifer Williams, who's in my house."

Elizabeth pushed away her plate. "Sorry. I suppose I should have known. Apparently that beastly child wrote her mother, who telephoned the head, who ticked me off, in a sort of nice, velvet-glove way."

"How maddening for you."

Sympathetic but noncommittal, Elizabeth thought. Playing safe with the head. And then, glancing into the older woman's candid brown eyes, she felt ashamed of her suspicion. "She was right, of course. Miss Geoffreys, I mean. I should have caught the whole mess early on.

What a tempest in a thimble! The trouble is—" She
paused. Miss Hinsley said nothing. Elizabeth stirred her
coffee. "The head seems to think I let it go, unconsciously anyway, because"—she stumbled over the de-
grading words—"I don't like Cecily."

"She *is* an irritating child, as everyone was saying in
the common room the other day."

"You weren't. You stick up for her. You even like her."

"Well, I do. I've talked to her once or twice alone.
When she isn't being defensive or showing off, she can
be intelligent and entertaining. She doesn't have the
standard reactions, and I find it refreshing. The other
evening at supper she conducted a solo defense of Oliver
Cromwell."

"Ugh," Elizabeth said.

"Yes, quite. That's what everyone else felt. And I'm
not at all sure she didn't elect herself devil's advocate
out of perversity and a fondness for argument. Of course,
it went to her head. She went on too long, lost her temper
and started to shout. I had to be sharp with her. But until then she was clear and original. I'm quite sure she
didn't get it out of the history book. She thinks for herself. She's different from the others in that way."

"She's that, all right," Elizabeth said. "Well, I'll try
and have a go at that side of her." She smiled faintly and
glanced at the wall clock. "We'd probably better get up.
Everyone's finished, and if we wait any longer your pro-
tegée will succumb to temptation and have another piece
of bread. She's eying it right now."

Miss Hinsley laughed and caught the eye of the head

girl. As the staff got up the rest of the school rose and waited while they filed out.

It was still raining after lunch. Games had been called off and the girls bundled in macs, berets and outdoor shoes and sent for a long walk though the fields and up to the beginning of the downs behind the school. A few of the hardier ones had organized a paper chase with the help of the gym mistress. Dressed in hockey shoes and thick white sweaters and carrying satchels of torn-up paper, the "hares" had started off, followed fifteen minutes later by the "hounds." They and the more sedate walkers had arrived back two hours later, red-cheeked, only moderately wet, and hungry for tea.

Elizabeth had spent the afternoon correcting compositions and checking last-minute details about the taxis ordered for six-thirty to take Miss Hinsley and the girls to the train for Mainbridge, their early supper, and the cocoa and bread and butter that would be waiting for them on their return.

At a quarter to five she marked her last composition B-minus, thought a bit, pulled a wry face, and crossed out the minus. Might as well give the child the benefit of the doubt of her own bad mood.

She pulled on a soft rose wool dress and shamefacedly added a drop of perfume to her ears, devoutly hoping she met no one on her way out. Tim had given her the perfume on her birthday.

She had been pleased and touched but had added, without thinking, "But I never wear scent."

He had grinned, unperturbed. "I know. But it's nice. And it does terrible things to the male."

So now she did, and wondered what her colleagues—and, for that matter, her father and brothers—would think of it. To her surprise she found she liked the elusive, insidious aroma. It made her feel luxurious and frivolous and unlike herself.

The rain had at last held up. Thank heaven, she thought, and headed down the curving, rhododendron-lined drive to the gates, reflecting that what with a new dress, the perfume and the providential cessation of rain her bad mood had vanished. But when she got to the gates she received a double shock: Against her express wishes Tim was there with his car, which was parked in the road. Tim himself was leaning against one of the stone posts, talking to Cecily Matthews.

Irritation that she knew to be out of proportion stung her.

"Cecily! What are you doing here?"

They both turned. Plainly they had not heard her coming. Cecily's animated expression hung for a second and then disappeared behind the familiar sullen look. "I was just taking a walk, Miss Marks."

Elizabeth opened her mouth and then hesitated. Until that moment she had assumed the child had slipped out against rules. Then she remembered that on Saturday afternoon, between tea and dinner, the girls were free to do more or less what they wanted. On fine days most of them put on their cloaks and wandered around the grounds—but not outside. Cecily was a few feet beyond the gates. Before she could stop herself Elizabeth said, "You realize you're out of bounds."

A mulish look came over Cecily's face. She stepped back inside the gates. "Sorry, Miss Marks. I hadn't noticed." Her voice held an exaggerated respect that barely escaped impudence.

Tim spoke up for the first time. "My fault, I'm afraid. I distracted her attention from the frontier." He smiled at both of them.

Elizabeth was furious—at Cecily, Tim and herself. She knew she was being both unjust and shrewish. An Englishman, brought up in English schools, would understand, she thought unfairly. She spoke to Cecily.

"Well, it's wet and you'd better run back now. You know how easily you catch cold." And, she added mentally, how much fuss your mother makes with her telephone calls and letters when you do. "You'll be having supper before leaving soon."

"Yes, Miss Marks." She turned to Tim and her face lit up again, this time with an added defiance. "Good-by, Mr. Nichols."

He gave her his pleasant smile. "Good-by, Cecily. Enjoy the play."

She drew the bulky cloak around her and started up the drive.

Tim straightened up and moved towards Elizabeth, smiling, his hands out. "Hi, darling."

She was embarrassed, intensely aware of the long rows of windows facing the gate, and moved quickly past his hands and out into the road. He looked a little surprised, dropped his hands, put them in his pockets and followed her.

She paused in the road, waiting for him to catch up, this time ready to return his greeting. But he merely strolled past and opened the door of the car for her. "Mademoiselle."

She got in and turned to face him. "I'm sorry, Tim. You know how I feel about your—your coming for me at the school. It's such a hive of gossip."

He closed the door without comment and went around the car to the driver's seat. Getting in, he closed it and started the car. "You sound a little like one of the girls breaking one of the rules. Since we are engaged, and they obviously know it, since you had to get permission to leave school early, I don't see why you should have this prejudice against my calling for you—particularly on a day like this when it's uncomfortable as well as inconvenient to get into Mainbridge. Wouldn't it be much more likely for them to think it damn peculiar if I didn't come?"

For the second time within the past few minutes—and the fourth time within the past few days—Elizabeth felt in the wrong. It was not a feeling she was accustomed to or liked. "You don't understand what a girls' school is like," she said stubbornly. "When the curate comes to tea the silly creatures erupt in giggles all over the place and go pink with excitement. Anything like this—" She stopped, unable to explain the look, probing, envious and intensely curious, that faced her across the classroom and the tables at meals. For some reason she had found it galling both to her pride and her sense of privacy.

"Well," he said genially, "I'm sorry. The next time you can get wet."

She glanced sideways at him through the gray, misty light.

His face was well put together, somewhat broader across the forehead and cheekbones than she was used to seeing. Without being strongly marked or particularly distinguished, it was a face people remembered. He had light brown hair, cut shorter than most Englishmen's, and gray eyes set rather deeply under the bones of his forehead. Used to her father, brothers and uncles, all of whom towered over six feet, Elizabeth was continually slightly surprised to see that Tim was of medium height only, standing level with her when she wore high heels. He was not stocky, but he looked strong.

The silence stretched between them. Elizabeth was not happy. The evening had started out badly. Tim didn't look angry and probably wasn't. He just meant what he said: the next time she could get wet—unless she apologized or said something to put things right. She was looking around for the right words when he said suddenly, "Why were you so sore at that kid?"

"Because she had no business being outside the gates and none whatever talking to you."

"Aren't you making a lot of fuss over a couple of feet? And why shouldn't she be talking to me? As a matter of fact I spoke first. She was there when I got out of the car, so I said 'hello.' "

Yes, he would, Elizabeth thought a little wryly, in his easy, casual transatlantic way. "I didn't know you had spoken to her first, but it doesn't make much difference. The girls are not supposed to talk to people they don't know. You could have been anybody."

"Oh, come now! She's not six years old. And I wasn't offering her candy."

"No," Elizabeth said, "she's not."

He glanced at her swiftly in the near darkness. "Great God, you're not jealous?"

For a second she wanted to hit him. Then she laughed. "Hardly. Don't be ridiculous. Good heavens, she's only thirteen—and unprepossessing, at that."

He grinned. "That's what I was telling you." And then added, "She's not a bad-looking kid. When she grows out of that puppy fat and learns what to do with her hair, she might be quite something. Her bones are good."

"What you can see of them."

"Give her time," he said easily. "What you need is a drink."

Genuine contrition overtook her. It suddenly occurred to her that frequently of late she had been bad-tempered and snapped at Tim. For a second she wondered why. In the first days of their courtship she loved the world. Now she was irritable, though she was more than ever aware of her love for him and for his seemingly endless good nature. On the other hand she knew she could neither bully nor push him. The puzzle nagged at her, its meaning hidden somewhere in Tim or within herself, where she couldn't find it. But now was no time to worry about it. The words she had been groping for came without effort.

"I'm sorry, Tim. I behaved rottenly."

"It's O.K." He leaned forward and wiped the sweating windscreen. "You're too cooped up in that female barrack. As I said, you need a drink."

She put her hand on his arm. "I think I need something else before that."

He steered the car into a cart track off the road, switched off the ignition, and gave her his full attention. Half an hour later they were on their way again. When they walked into the Mainbridge Inn she was ready to enjoy her drink, but she no longer needed it. Her face was soft, looking at the same time both younger and more mature. Her fair hair, curling in the damp, was a little untidy. Her pupils would not have recognized her. But Tim, sitting across the table from her in their booth, suddenly reached out and took hold of her hand. "Welcome back."

She stared at him over her drink. The liquor, but most of all the sensation that his love enveloped her, anesthetized some element of guarded pride. She was ready to dredge up admissions she never would otherwise have made. "I'm a pig, aren't I?"

He lit a cigarette. "No, darling. You're not a pig. But sometimes you seem—not hard—but as though your life or your virtue depended on upholding something that isn't really very important."

She leaned back, her head against the back of the settle. For some reason a picture from her childhood sprang vividly into her mind. She must have been very young, around eight. Because it was the last time she could remember going into one of her tantrums. She couldn't even be sure of the occasion. Something about a football. Oh, yes, her brothers were playing some four-man game of their own concoction. She wanted to join. They told her to buzz off. It was summer, because they were all home from school. Standing there in her cotton dress and sandals, she had felt rage coming at her like a massive wave and found herself screaming at them and stamping her feet. All four stopped playing. Without consultation they moved towards her, bore her kicking and yelling into the house, and, with the aid of chairs, shoved her onto the immensely high mantelpiece in the main hall. Then they removed the chairs and stepped back. Her eldest brother, Neil, said coldly, "If you can't learn to behave you can't play with us. When you've learned how to control yourself we'll get you down." And then they left.

After what seemed a long time her father walked through the room, a tall, black-haired man in a tweed jacket and boots. He noticed her and stopped. "What are you doing up there?"

She had reached the hiccuping stage, but her tears started up again. "Neil and the others put me up here."

He pulled out his pipe and started to pack it. "Why?"

"They wouldn't let me play with them." Her voice

rose on a wail. "It's not fair." She was sitting on the mantelpiece with her feet dangling over, and she started to pound the shelf with her fists.

He looked up from his pipe. "Stop that," he ordered. She stopped.

"Now," he said, "what's not fair? They're under no obligation to have you play with them—simply because you ask. There's nothing fair or unfair about it. If they invite you to join, then you can. If they don't, you shouldn't ask. Is that clear?"

It took her a while, staring into her father's unyielding hazel eyes. They were the color of the rocks at the bottom of the tarn, she thought. Then she dropped her gaze and said, "Yes."

Her father puffed at his pipe for a bit, then said, "Did they say they'd come and get you?"

She nodded.

"Then I dare say they will." He stood there, fifteen feet away, looking at her. He was so tall he could have lifted her down without even standing on his toes. "And if I ever see you indulge in another temper fit, you'll be confined to your room for a week. Do you understand?"

"Yes."

A glint of humor appeared in his eyes. "Fight for what you want if you must. But don't scream for it—that's a womanish trick."

She never knew if he spoke to the boys. She doubted it. An hour later, as good as his word, Neil appeared with Denis and lifted her down. He didn't speak to her or she to him. The matter was never referred to again.

Two days later, at considerable trouble and inconvenience to himself, Laurence Marks took his small daughter to a fair in the neighboring county. They stayed all day and she had a glorious time.

"What are you thinking about?"

Hearing in her ears the clipped, rather light accent and voice of her father, Tim's deep American voice seemed odd, out of place, for a moment. She straightened her head. "Something that happened when I was a bad-tempered little horror of eight."

He signaled the waiter and ordered another drink for them both. "Tell me about it."

"It's rather dull and there's not much point to it."

"I won't find it dull."

"All right," she said suddenly, "I will."

When she was through Tim stared at her a long time. "That was quite a Spartan upbringing you had. Freud certainly wouldn't approve."

"Freud was not English."

For a second he looked at her and then he laughed. He laughed at considerable length. "Spoken like Boadicea herself—and like your father. Do you really think if Freud could have had the advantage of an English upbringing the unconscious mind would have gone undiscovered?"

She smiled a little wryly. "No."

"One thing fascinates me. Obviously the greatest un-compliment your father could pay would be to call you womanish. What did he want you to be, manly?"

"He wanted me to learn pride and self-control."

He stubbed out his cigarette. "What was your mother like? Do you remember her at all?"

"Not too well. She was ill a long time before she died. I chiefly remember her being very beautiful and sitting up in bed." She paused for a second. "She was *warm.*"

"Do you remember when she died?"

She shook her head. "Not really. We were all sent away, and when we came back she wasn't there. I do remember at some point, when I first got back, I think, having an awful sense of desolation and thinking I couldn't bear it."

"And what did you do?"

She shrugged. "Bore it. What else was there to do?"

He pushed his glass around in a circle. "I still think your father was rather tough on you."

"Better too tough than not tough enough. Mollycoddled children are awful—can't stand on their own feet and lean all over other people. I can stand a really bad child, but I find that type unbearable."

"Like that Cecily whatever-her-name-is."

A little of the softness went out of her face. "Yes, like Cecily." Then defensively, "I'm not alone in my feeling, you know. No one likes her—neither staff nor girls."

"She must have a lonely time of it."

Elizabeth felt irritated. Why, no matter what she said, did it end up by Tim sympathizing with the child? "You know, considering what a blight she is and how difficult to cope with in the form, one would think you'd have a little sympathy for me—after all, you're a teacher yourself."

Tim smiled. "It's probably the fatal American tendency to take up for the underdog. No one seems to have a good word for the poor brat. Besides . . ." he hesitated and then grinned. "Whoever said England was a man's country was certainly right."

"What do you mean?"

"Because all the virtues you admire are the masculine ones—be tough, stand on your own feet, be a good sport, no mollycoddling. This is as true in your girls' schools as your boys', which is probably what made a Frenchman once say that the object of English schools for women was to turn out second-class men." He glanced up at her face. "Don't get mad, darling! You know I like England, but I assure you that this is the only country in the world where the peak of a girl's success is to be games captain."

She was staring down at her glass saying nothing, a slight frown on her face.

After a minute he went on. "More than anywhere else in the world, women in England take men at their own evaluation. That comes through in all your great novelists." He touched her hand. "And you, growing up in such a masculine household, got a double dose."

"Are American women different?" she asked.

He laughed. "Yes. Too much the other way. As a male, I find all this deference refreshing."

She looked up and smiled. "Even though it's against your principles to sympathize with me over Cecily?"

"Now who's violating principle? I thought you despised sympathy. You've just been telling me how you

were brought up not to indulge in such softness of character."

She said nothing but almost visibly retreated behind
her guarded façade.

Tim reached across the table and covered her hand
with his. "That was mean. What I meant to say was that
I don't think you're really that unrelenting. She certainly isn't the most promising material I've seen, but
you're too kind not to give the kid a break."

Elizabeth stared at him. "No, I'm not kind. Not in the
sense you are. I was brought up to be nice to animals and
the weak in the usual way. But I'm not kind. I'll try to
be, though." There was an unexpected humility in her
voice.

Tim slid out of his seat across from her and moved in
beside her. He pulled her to him and kissed her. "No
one can see us," he said reassuringly, and kissed her again.

Tim not only walked up the driveway with her to the
little brick house off the main school building that she
shared with various other staff members, but he kissed
her warmly and at some length on the doorstep. So far
from objecting, Elizabeth felt happy and pleasantly irre-
sponsible. "Just give me a chance," Tim muttered in her
ear, "and you won't have any moral character left."

Chuckling softly, she let herself in.

The main hall light had been turned off, leaving a
dim night light. Everything was quiet. Elizabeth was
therefore startled to see a light blazing under her own
door. Opening it, she went in and found Miss Hinsley

ensconced in her armchair, knitting, and a saucepan full
of cocoa warming in front of an open fire that had been
lit and was crackling busily. The older woman looked up.
"There you are," she said, in a low voice but as cheerfully
casual as though it were high noon. "I didn't think you'd
mind my waiting here for you, and I thought a fire and
some cocoa might be pleasant. It's so raw out."

Elizabeth was considerably surprised and her instinct
told her that something had happened. Her glow receded
but lay like a cushion against whatever tidings had
brought Miss Hinsley to wait. She slipped off her coat
and moved towards the old-fashioned wardrobe to hang
it up. On her way she caught sight of herself in her
dressing-table mirror and saw the dishevelment of her
hair. Reaching for a comb she smoothed it hastily, casting
a quick glance towards Miss Hinsley. But the latter had
bent down and was stirring the creamy brown liquid in
the pan. Had she noticed, Elizabeth wondered, or was it
tact? Not that it mattered a great deal. Still, annoyance
touched her faintly. She liked to present a closed, finished
front to the world—even a friendly one.

"Thank you for thinking of the cocoa," she said. "It is
a bit chilly."

Miss Hinsley eased back, somewhat red of face, and
pulled two cups down from the mantelpiece. Pouring in
the cocoa, she handed Elizabeth a cup and sat down in
the slightly smaller chair on the other side of the fire. It
was a fairly tight squeeze. "Did you and Tim have a
pleasant evening?"

"Yes, very." Elizabeth was a little nonplussed. It was

now midnight and about all she could say was that they had had dinner. "How was the play?" she asked hastily. "And thank you again for taking it on for me."

"Quite good. They stuck to the facts fairly well, even if they did give Pitt a slightly Byronic touch. And they made the most of the one romance he may or may not have had. The actor was far too good looking for the part, of course, and in the farewell scene I glanced down the row at twelve faces lost in the swamps of pure sentimentality." She sighed. "What a pity that a few moving facts about the evolution of Parliament can't evoke that rapt attention. Think how well they'd do on exams. They'll remember every word of those love scenes and sigh for weeks, but try and make one date stick."

Elizabeth's eyes twinkled a little. "And I suppose you sat there one solid block of granite—totally unmoved."

"You know I don't go in for that kind of slush," Miss Hinsley said. "It doesn't go with my age and figure." But her eyes smiled back in response.

Elizabeth sank down into the armchair. "Did our problem child navigate the evening successfully?"

"Well—no."

Elizabeth glanced up. She felt as if the child had been there like an albatross around her neck all evening. "Now what?"

"Not a great deal. And I don't think the girl can really be blamed for any of it. It's the usual story. When the taxis arrived the girls formed themselves into three groups —leaving her out. Naturally, I took her in the fourth taxi with me. The same kind of thing happened at the train. By this time sheer excitement had gone to their heads and they were giggling and shuffling around until I had to speak rather briskly to them. Jennifer sorted them out in a hurry and firmly added Cecily to one of the groups. She did it very well, not too obviously, but even so, somebody groaned, and you know what sheep they are at that age. They all turned around and stared at poor Cecily as though she had leprosy and then pointedly ignored her. There was nothing I could do. If I took her on the seat with me, it would be even more humiliating for her. But"—her voice hardened—"I shall speak to Jennifer and the other fourth formers in my house tomorrow. This kind of thing must stop at once. You can't force people to like someone. But this is cruelty and I won't have it. Of course"—she sighed a little—"Cecily was impossible after that. The rain had held up so we walked to the playhouse—it's only a few yards. Cecily made a great point of walking alone and lagged horribly, getting lost in the people behind us and frightening me out of my skin more than once. I couldn't even be sure she wouldn't just take off—and I must admit I wouldn't have blamed her if she had."

Like an evil spell, Cecily's name had banished the remnants of the evening for Elizabeth. She said suddenly, "What a pest she is! I wish her parents would take her out altogether and send her to another kind of school. She's not right for Langley and we certainly aren't right for her."

"You mean she doesn't conform to the type we go in

for—good family, good at games and an all-round good sport?"

Elizabeth frowned. "I don't quite follow you. Is there something wrong with what we try and do for the girls here?"

Miss Hinsley bent down and placed her empty cup on the tiles in front of the fireplace. "No, or I wouldn't still be here. Certainly not as long as Miss Geoffreys is running things." She leaned back and looked at Elizabeth. "The headmistress is a remarkable woman, and to me her most remarkable quality is that she does have time for individuals—even lumpy ones like Cecily."

Elizabeth felt a sense of shock. She had always liked the older woman and had taken it for granted that the older woman liked her. Now, suddenly, she wondered. "Are you trying to tell me that I don't like—individuals? That I want to turn the girls out like so many peas in a row? That's most unfair. You know the changes I made in English when I came here, letting the girls choose their own subjects for free composition and encouraging them to do research in the library on their own instead of the same dreary old set pieces, because I *do* believe that they learn more and do better if they're free to develop in their own way. And the school cert. results have proved me right."

"Yes, I know," Miss Hinsley said more gently. "But you don't have much room for the unprepossessing and the failures. And there's not much question: Cecily is a failure on almost any count you can think of."

"Well, it's her own fault."

"Partly, undoubtedly. And I'm not going to give you a lecture on the culpability of her parents. But she is a human being, she is unhappy, and—I'm sorry, my dear—I don't think you've ever bothered to find out if there's anything salvageable in her. There might be, you know. As I said to you the other morning, she's intelligent."

Elizabeth got to her feet and put her cup down on the mantelpiece with controlled care. "I seem to have heard nothing but Cecily, Cecily, Cecily all night long," she said.

Miss Hinsley looked startled. "From Tim?"

"Yes, from Tim. He came for me in the car, even though I had asked him not to, and when I arrived at the gate, who should be there talking to him and showing off but Miss Matthews herself."

Miss Hinsley looked at her curiously. "And what did Tim say about her?"

"He spent most of the evening sticking up for her and succeeded in making me feel like a cross between Mr. Murdstone and the village spinster."

"I like the sound of your young man. I'd like to meet him some time."

At any other time Elizabeth would have been pleased and touched at the comment. Now all she heard was the implied criticism. "Meaning—?"

Miss Hinsley stood up. "It's no use your getting annoyed with me, Elizabeth. I simply meant that your Tim sounded kind and tolerant. I'm very fond of you, my dear—I shouldn't be here if I weren't—but I think those are two qualities you would do well to work on."

The two women stared at each other in silence for a minute. "I think that's what Tim was trying to tell me earlier on," Elizabeth murmured.

"Well," Miss Hinsley said, "that brings me to my second note of cheer. Poor Miss Galloway had a slight heart attack tonight. It wasn't a bad one, and she'll be all right, but she certainly can't stay on as housemistress of St. Margaret's. Miss Geoffreys talked to me about it and said she'd decided to ask you to take it on for the rest of the term."

Elizabeth stood absolutely still. "Oh," she said. It was, of course, a great compliment. She would be the youngest mistress to be in charge of a house. And it was particularly reassuring after her last conversation with the headmistress. But that thought carried its own barb. With a rising sense of entrapment, she said, "That's Cecily's house, isn't it?"

Miss Hinsley nodded. "Yes. I'm afraid you're going to have to start exerting all your patience. For all that I feel sorry for her, she is a difficult child, and her mother's telephone calls and letters and complaints don't help. But"—she busied herself putting away her knitting—"I think if you can manage to put her on some kind of a road, give her some sense of direction, you'll be doing a lot. For yourself, as well as for her."

Elizabeth, who had relaxed and was listening, stiffened a little. "Naturally, I shall do my best for her, as for all the other thirty-odd girls in the house."

"Good," Miss Hinsley said firmly. "Well, good night,

my dear, I'll have to be getting back to my own house now before any of my own charges decide to run a fever or burn the place down or have a midnight feast. Good luck."

Elizabeth took the cups and saucepan and methodically washed them in the basin. Then she went and turned her bed down, her mind, for some reason, occupied with cataloging her achievements: she was only twenty-six and she had done very well in her career. She was senior mistress at one of the top-ranking boarding schools and now housemistress. She smoothed the sheet and the pillowcase. And she had worked hard for it, taking a first in English literature at Oxford, teaching for two years at another great school, and giving all she had when she came to Langley. She started to undress. Many of her pupils had done well on the Oxford and Cambridge entrance exams, and she got along well with her forms. She managed to be liked without being soft, and she got the most out of the girls in consequence. Miss Geoffreys, that wisest of women, liked her and had given her this new responsibility. Most of all, Tim loved her and would shortly take her back to America as his wife.

But as she slipped into her nightdress and let her mind rest on the bright future, she could not exorcise the sensation of having, somewhere, taken the wrong turning, the unshakable feeling that something was going very wrong.

"Damn the child," she suddenly said. In the quiet house it sounded like a shout, and she stood still, appalled,

to see if anyone had heard. But nothing stirred. She got
into bed and turned out the light.

Over in the South Dorm of St. Margaret's, Cecily lay
awake, her body rolled into a ball to try and generate
some warmth. All the windows were open, the heating
had clanked to a stop hours before, and the long, narrow
room was cold. The length of the room on one side was
divided by wooden partitions into six cubicles. Each one
contained a narrow bed, a dressing table with a mirror,
a chair and a wash basin with running water. Curtains
could be pulled across the front of the cubicles, and
across a narrow aisle, directly opposite, were the shallow
cupboards where blouses, skirts, jackets and gym tunics
were hung over a shelf containing, for each girl, a pair
of indoor shoes, a pair of outdoor shoes, gym shoes and
dancing slippers.

When the four girls from St. Margaret's who had been
to the play returned, they found their beds turned down
and their hot water bottles filled. After the miserable
journey to Mainbridge and the bitter intervals when
everyone seemed to talk around and over but never to her,
Cecily had felt sick all the way home, convinced that her
bed would be untouched and her hot water bottle empty
and cold. When she found this to be untrue, ready emotion welled up in her. She felt friendly and wanted to
talk to someone, to let it be known, casually, that this had
been done for her. But lights had been out for hours and
everyone was asleep. Undressing quickly and getting into
bed, she pulled the hot water bottle up in the crook made

by her bent knees and concentrated on warming up. As warmth started to flow through her, her mind, recoiling a little here and there, went back over the evening.

The memory of her conversation at the school gate with Miss Marks's young man was like a bright light in a dark alley. Curling her toes a little, she let a slight shiver pass over her. Without a thought, she abandoned the current image of her beau ideal—the dark, dramatic, towering hero who had always moved about in the misty background of her mind, suitably garbed for his time and role: in eighteenth-century dress, with a dueling sword; with rope and ax, scaling the frozen heights (this was after a lesser but handsome young mountaineer had been induced to give a Saturday afternoon lecture at the school); immaculate in striped trousers and black jacket, arriving at the school with the announcement that both her parents had been, most unfortunately, killed in an accident and he placed in charge of her upbringing. At which point, of course, he would remove her from the school, after several coldly stated criticisms of the treatment afforded her, to the envy of everyone from Miss Geoffreys down. He was of mysterious though obviously aristocratic origin. On one side of his family he was half Scottish and half Spanish. On the other. . . . Cecily had worked out every detail of his parents, his kinsmen and his life from the time of his (illegitimate) birth on. The facts, of course, changed from time to time, according usually to what she had recently read. But he was always in her mind, most vividly, of course, at night, when she could concentrate on him: her father, her friend, her lover, her confidant, her ally, in the mirror of whose im-movable and undeviating love she saw herself as forever lovable and different, in every particular, from the image that the world, and most especially she herself, had of her.

Nevertheless now, without a pang, she killed him off. Into his place moved the far more physical presence of Timothy Nichols.

Sighing a little, she turned over, twisting until she had the bedclothes wrapped, cocoon-like, around her. She went over their brief conversation, word by word, savor-ing the memory of his exotically slurred vowels. She would make a great point, from now on, of studying what little of American history was offered in the school cur-riculum. In fact— Her imagination soared.

And then Miss Marks had arrived. The old charm of the goddesslike young woman asserted itself. The very scorn she showed towards Cecily was an attraction. She was a fitting mate, Cecily felt, for her new hero. And yet— Resentment, gathering power, pushed through her as she relived the humiliating scene after the mistress had arrived. She felt her own lumpy unworthiness and hated the teacher for it. And now the miseries of the rest of the evening marched forward: the giggles, the whispers she couldn't hear, the ones she could, the silent, staring faces, Miss Hinsley's searing kindness.

She turned again, drawing up her legs. Mr. Nichols— Timothy (her heart beat a little faster)—would show them all, particularly Miss Marks. One afternoon, on a half holiday, he would simply come up to the school and ask if he could take Cecily Matthews out for the afternoon. When asked why, he would say that he found her attractive, intelligent and sympathetic beyond anyone he'd met in a long time. He would . . .

She fell asleep.

3

TAKING OVER in mid-term would not have been easy anyway. But after the first few days, Elizabeth's respect for the combined vigilance and wisdom of a successful housemistress went soaring up.

"How on earth do you do it?" she said one day to Miss Hinsley in the common room. "Simply teaching English and nothing else seems by comparison now a sybaritic life."

Miss Hinsley poked the fire. "You'll get used to it. It's like everything else. After a while you develop a sixth sense."

"You need to. I've already learned that at least a third of them can't be believed when telling you how they are this morning, thank you."

Miss Hinsley laughed. "Yes, I know, all too well! Some will lie themselves blue to get out of games, school, or anything at all except lie in the sickroom and read. And then there are those who won't admit anything's wrong until you've discovered they've passed out with a fever of a hundred and three!"

"Exactly. But before I've learned the difference I'll probably have killed off half a dozen."

"Not likely. You've a good head on your shoulders.

You should be able to tell when someone's not up to par, whatever her tongue is saying." She paused and glanced at the pretty young woman slumped—no, Miss Hinsley thought wryly, Elizabeth would never slump—relaxed in a chair. "How's the problem child?"

"Quiescent, thank God." But there was something in her voice, or on her face, that made Miss Hinsley ask:

"Anything wrong?"

Elizabeth shook her head. "No." She started to open her mouth again when the school bell went. She pushed herself up and picked up her pile of books. "If I'm not worrying about their bowels I am about their school cert. and entrance exams!" She cast an ironic glance heavenwards and started towards the door.

Miss Hinsley said quickly, "Everything all right, Elizabeth?"

A bare pause, then, "Yes, of course." Elizabeth smiled politely.

"Because if there's anything at all I can do. . . . I mean, if you should want to talk something over, or—" For the first time in many years the older woman found herself foundering.

"Kind of you. But everything seems to be going quite well. Pure good luck, I'm sure." And with the same polite smile she went out and closed the door.

Miss Hinsley sat and stared at the fire. I wonder, she thought, if I should go and see Miss Geoffreys? And then, what good would it do? Her practical mind repudiated anything hinging on superstition. Yet she couldn't get rid of an uneasiness. Outside the rain lashed against the windows and blew in wild circles around the dark, slippery trees. Drops fell down the chimney and hissed into the fire. I wish it were May, she thought. I wish her young man were going to take her away now. She was astonished and upset at how strongly she felt about it.

The following morning was Friday. The rain had stopped, but the sky was gray and the wind, no longer hampered by its burden of rain, snarled around the edges of the windows and doors. It was impossible to keep warm.

Elizabeth, now installed in St. Margaret's, was in her private sitting room following breakfast. It was now, for her, the most trying meal of the day, the one at which she eyed her charges most carefully, trying to decide who was about to come down with a cold, flu, measles, stomach ache or any other ailment. This morning she had come to the conclusion that under the electric light, which the dark outside made necessary, they all looked dreadful. She was busy sorting out the mail when there was a knock at the door.

"Come in."

The door opened to reveal Cecily's ample form. She seemed to be breathing heavily and was clutching a large, moist-looking handkerchief. Elizabeth was suddenly aware of her own freshness, of her cool, slim, well-proportioned body. "Yes, Cecily?" she said pleasantly.

"I think I'm getting a bad cold, Miss Marks."

Elizabeth tried to decide whether the adenoidal stickiness of the consonants was put on or genuine. "Let's see if you have any fever." Taking a thermometer out of its cup of sterilizer she shoved it into the child's mouth. "Just leave it there for a minute and don't talk. You can sit down," she added.

Cecily went to a chair and sat down. The lamp above her poured light down on her head. Elizabeth, glancing over, saw the shine on the straight brown hair and the red glints in it. Cecily's mouth, clamped around the thermometer, was twisted out of shape, but her forehead rose smooth and vertical, forming a sharp angle with the straight, strong nose. Letters in hand, Elizabeth glanced at her and thought idly, Tim's right, she has good bones. The tense thread of hostility seemed to relax suddenly. I wonder why they hate her, really, Elizabeth thought. And then, with a pang, Or why I do? I'll have a talk with the child, I'll—

Cecily suddenly put up her hand, pulled out the thermometer and peered at it.

"What on earth—?" Elizabeth strode over. "I did not tell you to take it out of your mouth," she said disapprovingly. "Really, Cecily. Put it straight back in and keep it there until I tell you you can remove it."

"Sorry, Miss Marks." She put it back in.

Elizabeth finished sorting the letters, glanced at the clock and, going over, took the thermometer. "You haven't any fever at all," she said.

"But I feel awful."

Elizabeth glanced down at Cecily. Her color was good and not too high. She looked perfectly well, even though she obviously had caught a slight cold.

"Nonsense. Eat lightly today."

"Do I have to go to school?"

Elizabeth noticed that she sounded less adenoidal. "Yes, of course you do. Don't be so lazy, Cecily."

"But I don't feel a *bit* like going to games." The sticky consonants had returned.

Elizabeth opened her mouth to assure her on this point as well when caution, however unwelcome, intervened. The wretched child *did* have a cold. "You needn't go to games, but exercise and fresh air will do your cold good, not harm. Wrap up warmly and take the walk with Miss Reynolds."

The round face fell. "But don't you think I ought to sit by the fire—?"

"And read lazily, which is what you would really like to do all day every day? No, Cecily. You may not. Stop making such a fuss over yourself. You make more fuss than all the others combined in St. Margaret's. Now run along or you'll be late."

Deliberately she turned her back. Cecily's feet clattered solidly down the corridor.

"How's my little friend, Cecily?" Tim asked the following evening.

"Wheezing like a grampus in a grandstand effort to make me let her stay at the house and slack instead of going to school or—heaven forbid—play games."

Tim laughed. "She wouldn't be much on the playing field. Not with that girth. But why does she hate school? What are her marks like?"

"Frightful." She paused. "Oddly enough, about the first two months she was at the school she did extremely well. Came out top in everything. Read off on the honors list every Monday morning. So she got promoted from the lower to the upper fourth form and has done nothing but come out bottom and fail everything, practically, ever since."

"Is there that much difference between the two forms?"

"I wouldn't have thought so."

"Then it must be something else."

"Well, she had a first flush of popularity too. She used to make funny remarks that set everyone laughing, until she got bumptious and they started sounding pseudo-funny instead and all at once everyone found her brash and impossible."

"Unsure of herself, went too far, and now can't do anything right. Is that it?"

"I suppose so. You seem to have it down very pat."

"Have you ever heard of a pecking order?"

"No. What on earth's that?"

"It's something animals, hens and so on, set up. A hierarchy of authority. When a new member arrives, depending on how well and firmly he stands up for himself, he gets stuck somewhere along the line of rank, and everyone above him, from then on, can pick on him all they want. He can pick on those below. It seems like Cecily, by bad timing, got herself shoved to the bottom. And in a primitive world—which a child's world is—once you've become established as an outlaw, God himself couldn't change your status." Abruptly he glanced up. "Do you like her any better?"

"No, I don't. And I'm tired of talking about her."

He grinned. "Sorry."

She looked at him for a minute. "Just as a matter of curiosity, is there any boy at that establishment of yours that, despite all the fairness you try to exert, you can't like?"

"Yes. A lad named David Allenby. The exact opposite in every way from your Cecily. Bright, on the cricket team, good-looking and a cold, self-satisfied s.o.b.—if you'll pardon the expression." He laughed suddenly. "I think your father would have approved of him. I've never seen him lose face or control. There he is, in perfect command of the situation, baiting some other poor kid into impotent rage."

"And you think my father would approve of somebody who sounds like a first-class bully? I don't greatly appreciate that, Tim. Of all the—"

He put his hand out quickly. "I'm sorry, darling. No, I didn't mean that. Or at least"—he paused—"not entirely. But from what you said, he would have had even less sympathy for the boys who let themselves be pushed around."

For a second Elizabeth paused, her hand under his. Then she pulled it away. "I'm afraid we seem destined to disagree on this." She lit a cigarette. "Let's talk about something else, shall we? Or had I better go home?"

She could feel the shaking inside her and knew, with a small, detached portion of her mind, that she was de-

liberately allowing this quarrel to take place; that the
nervous strain of the past few weeks had built up a res-
ervoir of anger which was now rising to the surface. It
would have been possible to quarrel on other occasions.
There had always been differences. But on other occasions she had exerted a conscious effort of understanding,
which she was not exerting now.

Tim hesitated a moment. Was he, too, not completely
trying? "Do you want to?" he asked. "Go home, I mean."

Now she wanted him to talk her out of it, to give her
reassurance. She waited, but the question hung in the
air.

"Perhaps we'd better," she said coolly. "It's getting late
anyway." She started to pull her coat on, and after watching her a few seconds Tim came around and helped her.

Silently they left the restaurant and got into his car,
and silently he drove her back to the school. Pride kept
her from talking, but not from wishing that he would
break through the wall that had sprung up so suddenly.
Or had it? Had it been in the making a long time?

He pulled the car up about ten yards from the gates.
"I know how it embarrasses you for me to take you to the
door. So since I can't seem to do anything right tonight,
I'll leave you here."

It was an acid pill to swallow. Since the time he had
come for her on the rainy day, she had grown used to
his escorting her to the house—and had come to like it.

"Thank you," she said stiffly, and climbed out. Tim got
out the other side.

She stood there in the chilly evening, shivering from

cold and misery. "Well, good night, Tim. Thank you for the evening."

He bowed with grave formality. "Thank you."

He stood a few feet from her. She tried to scan his face in the dark, to see if he was unhappy or simply angry; whether he cared. And at that moment it began to dawn on her dimly that her own control, on which she so prided herself, was a flimsy affair compared to his; that he was one of those deceptively friendly and re- laxed people, but that his reticence lay deep and well hidden. It was a disturbing thought and she pushed it from her. "Good night, then," she said, as though he were another teacher or a casual acquaintance, and walked briskly up the drive.

She lay awake for a long time. Tim had been so in- tegral a part of her life for nearly half a year that she felt now as though she had suffered an amputation. They had seen each other every Saturday night for months. It had become a matter of course. But he had not actually said anything about the coming week, nor did he mention having a quick dinner in between, which they had lately fallen into the habit of doing.

Monday brought its own dish of gloom in the form of a letter from Mrs. Matthews, who was outraged that Cecily, suffering from a cold, had not only been forced to attend school but to go on a walk. *Cecily has always got colds easily,* the slightly hysterical letter stated, *and her colds often turn into something serious, like bron- chitis. She shouldn't be allowed to go out or even sit in*

the draughty schoolrooms. If you can't take proper care
of her I shall have to write to Miss Geoffreys. I know,
of course, that you're new as housemistress, but. . . .
The letter circled back to its original topic twice more.

Her nerves raw to begin with, Elizabeth had to struggle with herself for several minutes before she could
open the rest of her mail. When she had calmed a little,
she reviewed the glimpses she had had of Cecily through
the week end. Her cold had seemed no worse. And several other matters had cropped up to distract Elizabeth's
attention. One of those distractions—Ann Rodney—now
crossed Elizabeth's mind again. She had caught sight of
the girl at Sunday dinner and, even from her own position at the high table where the staff sat, had been able
to see that the ebullient Ann was looking a little droopy.
That evening at supper Elizabeth, sitting at the end of
the house table, saw that Ann's usually rosy cheeks were
looking a little pasty and that she picked at her food.
She had cornered her after the meal.

"Are you all right, Ann? You look a little seedy to me."

"Oh, yes, Miss Marks," Ann said with great emphasis.
"I just wasn't very hungry tonight." Elizabeth was not
completely reassured but, when she saw Ann chattering
animatedly in the sitting room later, decided she was
telling the truth.

Elizabeth got up and propped open her sitting room
door, so that she could see the girls as they passed, head-
ing towards the passageway and the school building. She
had barely sat down when Cecily appeared.

"Yes?" Elizabeth said. She tried not to think about Mrs. Matthews's letter.

"My cold is no better and I feel absolutely awful." Her face contorted, she rummaged into her blazer pocket and pulled out a grimy looking handkerchief, but not in time. A large, wet sneeze shook her.

"Try not to give everyone else your cold," Elizabeth said. And then, because she was not Cecily's form mistress for nothing, "Have you done all your homework for today, Cecily?"

"Bost of it." Again, Cecily's adenoidal condition might, or might not, have been genuine.

Elizabeth repressed a sigh. She was strongly tempted to send Cecily off to school, to games and to every other activity of the day. Others didn't catch cold with the same maniacal frequency. Probably because they were less coddled. A good stint of toughening up would probably produce a shower of colds, but would cure her. All of Elizabeth's instincts pushed her in this direction. But the wretched Mrs. Matthews's letter, with its threat, hung at the back of Elizabeth's mind. Cecily was already a problem between her and the headmistress. She had slipped once and her pride had been damaged. It hurt now to realize that she was allowing herself to be blackmailed by a hysterical mother. Yet—

Hopefully she took Cecily's temperature again. If it had gone up even one half of a degree, her pride would be justified. But it hadn't. Nevertheless—

"Very well, Cecily. Go to the sickroom and get into

bed. I'll come in after a while and give you an aspirin. Perhaps a day there will cure this."

Cecily's face noticeably brightened. "Yes, Miss Marks. I'll just get my hot water bottle."

"Do," Elizabeth said dryly.

Lazy little pig, she thought, and sat down again.

There was a clatter of shoes and a swift, blue-serged form flew past the open door.

"Ann," Elizabeth called out.

The shoes slid to a stop and came slowly back.

"Yes, Miss Marks."

"Ann, how do you feel this morning?" Elizabeth's mind suddenly went back to Miss Hinsley's statement. She would almost have to bludgeon Ann to get an accurate answer.

"I feel fine, Miss Marks. Super, in fact."

Elizabeth looked at her. Ann's color was normal again. But there was something about her eyes and the look of her skin that made Elizabeth feel vaguely uncertain. "Are you really telling me the truth? Do you really feel up to par?"

Ann's urchin smile appeared. "Rather!"

I should put her in the sickroom and have Dr. Harwood in to see her, Elizabeth thought. Then she remembered that by now Cecily would be there. The sickroom, a temporary haven for minor ailments, contained only one bed. Anyone more seriously ill was dispatched to the sanatorium under the charge of the school nurse. To send Ann, waiting now with polite but visible impatience, to the sanatorium because of nothing more than a vague uneasiness, seemed extreme and absurd. "All right, Ann. But you must promise to come straight back here if you don't feel well today."

"Yes, Miss Marks. I will."

She was off, going down the stairs two at a time. Elizabeth smiled. She liked Ann, no great student, only good enough at hockey to have made the second team, but lively, candid and game. Not a square corner there. No unpredictabilities. No instabilities. She suddenly paused in the act of arranging the morning delivery of letters to wonder what Tim would think of Ann. Probably he would like her well enough but think her only moderately interesting. She could hear his voice say "healthy, well-adjusted schoolgirl."

Elizabeth smiled to herself, but there was pain in it. She had hoped he would telephone her Sunday and had stayed around her room as much as she dared so she could hear the ring. But he hadn't telephoned. And she was not quite ready to entertain the idea that she would have to make the first move. Of course, he had apologized. Even so, he had insulted her father. The old anger and irritation arose. She pushed the problem out of her mind.

The day wore on. Elizabeth dropped into the sickroom, gave Cecily an aspirin, noted that the child not only looked pretty well but in far better spirits than usual, sitting up in bed, wheezing slightly and devouring one of the four books she had on the bed.

"I think you'd better be on a light diet today," Elizabeth took extraordinary pleasure in saying. "Soup for lunch, and some fish perhaps for dinner. If you don't feel well, you probably don't have much appetite," she added with a touch of malice. Cecily's face had fallen. Plainly there was nothing much wrong with her appetite.

In the afternoon Elizabeth wrapped herself in her coat and joined one or two other staff members down at the games field to see St. Margaret's play St. Jean's. Ann, who played center forward, had already scored two goals. Watching her race up and down the field, Elizabeth wondered for the first time if the afternoon's match had anything to do with Ann's hearty assurances of health. The thought was so obvious that Elizabeth's doubt and uncertainty grew. But the girl looked all right and was plainly enjoying herself.

Elizabeth took another close look at her that night when she went into the North Dormitory to turn off the lights. I'll tackle her again tomorrow morning, she thought, and if there's any doubt at all I'll have old Harwood over.

"All right, Ann?"

This time there was a slight pause. "Yes, Miss Marks."

Elizabeth went and stood at the end of the narrow bed. "Sure?"

"Yes, Miss Marks." But she didn't sound quite so convinced. Elizabeth bent over and felt Ann's neck and head. They seemed normal. "I think I'll have the doctor look you over tomorrow," she said firmly. "Good night, everyone." She clicked off the light and closed the door.

*   *   *

Elizabeth was a light sleeper and waked immediately when there was a knock on her door and she heard the voice of one of the prefects, Sue Parsons, outside. Sue was head of the North Dormitory. Ann, Elizabeth thought, in that instant between getting out of bed and going to the door.

"It's Ann," Sue said, with the implacable calm of a good prefect. "She seems in awful pain and she's all doubled up. She called Pat Holmes, who is in the next cubicle, and Pat called me." And suddenly, absurdly, Elizabeth saw in this moment of emergency the chain of command from the smallest junior up to Miss Geoffreys.

She snatched up her robe. "I'll come right away."

The dormitory was by this time well awake, though Sue used her authority to quell the smaller, younger members and get them back to their own beds. "Eileen, has anyone given you permission to get out of bed? Valerie, what are you doing up?" Like a whip at a fox hunt she restored order.

Elizabeth went straight to Ann's bed. There was no question about her condition: she was lying with her knees up, her hands pressed against her abdomen. Frightened eyes stared back at the teacher from a pinched, white face.

Fear clutched at Elizabeth and for a few seconds rooted her to the floor. Suddenly the whole responsibility seemed too much. Then training—and compassion—came to her rescue.

She bent over the bed. "Hang on, Ann. I'm going to ring the doctor. I'll be as quick as I can. Try not to worry. I know it's ghastly, but it probably feels worse than it is." She smiled with all the reassurance she could summon and saw the panicky look in the girl's eyes recede. Briefly, she rested her hand on Ann's head. Then she turned. "Sue, stay here. I'm ringing Dr. Harwood and Miss Geoffreys."

She telephoned the doctor, rousing him from his sleep. "All right," he said when he had listened to her for a few minutes. "I'll be over." Plainly he was reluctant. He was elderly and the night was cold and he was never quite convinced that a lot of silly women, cooped up together, would not give in to foolish imaginings. But the school was, first, a profitable part of his practice and, second, his responsibility.

Then Elizabeth rang Miss Geoffreys.

It was two hours later by the time the doctor had come, been startled into a swift diagnosis, and sent for the ambulance from the local hospital.

Miss Geoffreys had long since arrived, her regal dignity unimpaired by her appearance in a long dark-red woolen dressing gown, her abundant gray hair in its night-time plait twisted up into a bun.

With the noise of the ambulance backing up to the door and the unusual sound of men's voices in the hallways, Elizabeth gave up all hope of keeping the bulk of her thirty-odd charges behind the closed doors of their own dormitories. Pajama-clad figures appeared in doorways, the taller ones topped by heads glinting with pins and improvised curlers. "Get back into your bedrooms, all of you," Elizabeth said automatically, while guiding the two stalwart young stretcher-bearers through the labyrinths to the North Dorm.

Miss Geoffreys was sitting on a straight chair beside Ann's bed and was holding her hand. Elizabeth, her sensitivity and observation sharpened by tension, noticed that she managed to do this as though it were the most natural—even obvious—thing to do. And Ann, for all her usual modish disdain for show of sentiment, looked very glad to have Miss Geoffreys there. With all the commotion her fright had returned, and the appearance of two young men in white surgical coats, carrying a stretcher, did not help.

Miss Geoffreys saw Ann's slight recoil. "Now, Ann," she said in a quiet voice. "You're going to the hospital where they'll take your appendix out so that it won't give you any more trouble. You'll go on a stretcher because that way will joggle and hurt you least, and Miss Marks is going with you. I'm afraid, Ann dear, you'll be rather uncomfortable for a day or two, but you have nothing more serious to worry about than that." Her remarkable smile, with its warmth, affection and assurance, almost visibly poured strength back into the girl.

Elizabeth, watching, felt young and raw and inadequate. The awe in which she had always held the headmistress—somewhat dimmed of late by her sense of having lost the older woman's approval—returned. She is a great lady, Elizabeth thought.

Miss Geoffreys stood up and moved out of the cubicle as the stretcher-bearers slid Ann onto the stretcher and covered her with a blanket.

Elizabeth, who had managed to get into some clothes, turned to follow the men downstairs.

"Miss Marks."

Elizabeth turned back. "Yes, Miss Geoffreys?"

The older woman smiled once more, and Elizabeth suddenly realized that she herself must look as frightened as one of the pupils, because she could feel the contrasting sense of reassurance.

"The main thing is to keep Ann's mind off her woes. She's a sensible child and it shouldn't be too difficult. Telephone me as soon as they have finished operating."

To her own intense annoyance, Elizabeth found herself confessing, "I feel I should have known something was seriously wrong with Ann. She's looked seedy for a day or two, now, but swore to me she felt all right. I think she wanted to play in that match this afternoon. But I should have known better than to take her word."

"My dear, you can't be expected to know straight off how far to take a child's word and how much to trust your own judgment. You'll develop an instinct, but it takes time and you've barely started." The headmistress moved down the hall beside Elizabeth. "And now, when you've got Ann safely settled, get yourself a hot drink— and if someone offers you something alcoholic, I shouldn't turn it down."

Elizabeth felt as she had as a small child when she had gone on hill climbs with her father and brothers. At the end of a difficult day, and if he thought his daughter had done her full share without complaining, Colonel Marks would place his hand against the small of her back, not exactly pushing her up a steep hill but holding, so that her own weight seemed less.

Miss Geoffreys turned at the head of the stairs. "Now, off you go. I shall go and telephone Ann's parents." A different, almost mischievous smile broke over her features. "At least I can be grateful they're not the Matthews." With a nod she moved down the staircase and through the door leading to the passageway and the main building.

Downstairs, the men were negotiating the front steps. Elizabeth went quickly back into the North Dorm, her brogues slapping the floor briskly. There were a few hasty scuffles. "Everyone in bed?" she asked.

"Yes, Miss Marks." Sue Parsons's voice sounded as if she knew what she was talking about.

Elizabeth switched off the lights and went back into the center hall. Further scuffles made her glance swiftly at the three half-open dormitory doors above the stair well. She was about to repeat her question when the name "Matthews," dropped a few minutes previously by the headmistress, seemed suddenly to register. She glanced at the sickroom door, some thirty feet away. How, until now, she could have missed Cecily's rotund bulk wrapped in a blue dressing gown and peering through the sickroom door with avid interest, Elizabeth didn't know. But at the sight of the child the tension of the previous weeks, the fearful strain of the past few hours and her sense of overburdened responsibility collided explosively within her in the kind of rage she had known only once or twice in her life. She made no attempt to go up to Cecily. Her voice covered the distance.

"Cecily Matthews, since you spent such a length of time convincing me what a dreadful cold you had and how delicate you were, I would think your tender regard for yourself would keep you from lounging around a drafty hall, even at the cost of missing something that is none of your concern, anyway."

She could hear her voice, carrying, half an octave higher than usual and whittled sharp. With total clarity she recalled the words of the first headmistress she had served under. *Never use sarcasm on a child. For one thing, it's a cheap weapon. For another, the child can't answer back.* But she couldn't stop herself. A powerful tide that had its origins in the past was pushing her.

"And it might interest you to know, further, that if you hadn't made such a fearful fuss about getting into the sickroom where you could laze for a while, Ann might have been there yesterday. The doctor would probably have seen her, and this whole miserable night's work could have been avoided."

Cecily's mouth was slightly open. Pure shock had immobilized her. She stared at the tall, furious, beautiful young woman who seemed to carry a sword in her hand and a pair of flaming wings on her back. From the rooms above and around, stray whispers reached her ears. She glanced in their direction. Dormitory doors open, heads piled in the doorways, half of St. Margaret's had heard the housemistress's stinging reproof. The fact that the last part of it was only technically true and completely unjust was something that neither they, nor Cecily herself, knew. Only Elizabeth was dimly aware of it.

After a paralyzed few seconds, Cecily took half a step forward, then shrank back and closed the door.

Through her ebbing fury Elizabeth became conscious of the large, though now rapidly vanishing, audience, of the twenty-odd average, good-hearted, unthinking, cruel possessors of the half lie she had used like a machete on the wretched Cecily. She also became aware that by this final act, whether unconsciously she did or did not know about the listeners, she had stepped across some line.

"Everyone must shut the door and go to bed *immediately*," she called out sharply. She heard the doors close.

"Are you coming, Miss Marks?" It was Dr. Harwood. "We've got Ann safely in."

So this last, terrible scene had just taken a few seconds. For the second time she felt torn between the two children, but this time her instincts had crossed to the other side. I should go and see if Cecily's all right, she thought.

"That appendix isn't going to wait forever, Miss Marks."

"All right, I'm coming."

Elizabeth plunged down the stairs. She felt that for the first time in her well-ordered life she was showing a talent for making the wrong decisions.

4

AT ELEVEN o'clock Saturday morning Tim rang up. Throughout the miserable, limping week Elizabeth, already distracted by worry about Ann and Cecily and her handling of the house as a whole, had vacillated between her leftover anger at Tim and a growing fear that she would not see him; that his chilly farewell the previous Saturday had been final. He had not telephoned for a midweek dinner. What with visiting Ann in the hospital whenever she could snatch a free hour, she couldn't have gone if he had. But it would have allayed both her anger and her fear. By Friday she allowed herself to think about telephoning him. But her elaborate array of reasons did not get too far in convincing her own inner faculty for self-candor. She wanted to ring him because she wanted to ring him, and she knew it. Pride and a busy schedule had kept her from doing so. By the time her telephone rang Saturday morning she was tired, tense and actively unhappy.

"When and where do you want to meet?" Tim asked without too much preamble.

Elizabeth hesitated, part of her longing to give herself the luxury of a show of cool surprise and the statement that she had made other plans, another part yearning to give in to reproach. But prudence, the fear of pushing his easy but by no means soft nature too far, was the strongest. She hesitated before speaking, wishing, and astonished at herself for doing so, that he would offer to call for her. With a pang she remembered the times he had come against her wishes. Now she felt that to have the world at large see him call for her would do a lot for her morale. "Would you like to meet at the inn?" she finally asked.

"All right. What time?"

Disappointed, she replied, "Six thirty."

"See you then," Tim said, and rang off. Elizabeth hung up slowly, recalling now, also, the times she had quashed his attempts to whisper mild affections over the telephone. Unfamiliar doubts pricked at her consciousness: doubts about herself and, by extension, about attitudes and ideas which she had never really questioned. The fabric of her life and beliefs had been totally consistent with each other, invisibly woven into solid cloth. Now—if you pulled one thread, questioned one part, the whole became fallible. Seven hours, she thought dismally, until she could see Tim.

That afternoon she went to visit Ann, who was recovering rapidly and whose cheerful good spirits were dampened only by the thought of the three remaining house matches she would not be able to play. Amused and sympathetic, Elizabeth condoled with her. Later, returning to the school, her amusement took a slightly wry turn. As she got off the bus and started to climb the slow hill up to the school it struck her that Ann was, in basic type,

the kind of child she herself had been. And dealing with
her was no problem. I could cope, she thought, with a
school full of Anns for the rest of my life and not put a
foot wrong. For a moment she longed for the simpler,
less demanding time before Cecily—and even Tim—had
come into her life. And then she realized that during the
past weeks the two had become bracketed in her mind.
It jolted her and brought back the depression of the
morning.

It was after tea that she passed the door of the house
sitting room and was almost thunderstruck to find Cecily
sitting with her back to the wall in the corridor outside,
her feet stuck out in front of her. By school rule the
pupils neither lingered nor talked—let alone sat—in the
cold hallways. Elizabeth would have been no more
amazed to find Cecily walking on her hands. As it was,
she almost fell over her feet.

"What on earth are you doing here?" she demanded.

Cecily drew her legs under her and rose cumber-
somely. "Nothing, Miss Marks," she said after a pause.

The answer was so palpably absurd that Elizabeth was
stopped for a minute. She tried to see Cecily's face, but
the light was dim. "Do you mean to say that for some—
incredible—reason you simply decided to sit down in the
corridor?"

Cecily looked straight back at her but said nothing.

Elizabeth's nerves tightened with irritation. But she
hesitated. Her teacher's instinct scented trouble. Abruptly
she turned the knob of the door and walked in.

About a dozen girls were grouped around the fire, the

tall, copper head of Audrey Leach in the center. Like
trapped conspirators they half turned, mouths partly open.
Then they all wheeled and smiled politely. They were
what the staff called the middle-aged group, fifteen-year-
olds—probably the most difficult age of all to deal with.
The sight of Audrey gave Elizabeth a pang of disquiet.
She knew the girl had a talent for minor cruelty and a
gift for making others play along.

The silence lengthened unpleasantly. Surprised, Elizabeth realized that she was facing a battle of wills between
herself and the girl, Audrey. She waited for the confidence, the efficient dominance that had always enabled
her to control such moments. But something had gone
wrong. She wracked her mind and called on her experi-
ence, but she could think of nothing, no way to break
the deadlock. Yet she knew something had happened,
that Cecily had been pushed or driven from the common
sitting room. Defeated, her eyes turned away.

"What is that book doing on the floor?" she said finally.
All eyes turned to the open book lying face down on the
carpet. There was no response. The girl nearest to it bent
down and picked it up, placing it on the table behind her.

Her voice cold, Elizabeth demanded, "To whom does
it belong?"

A detached voice spoke up. "It's Cecily's, Miss Marks."

"And who threw it on the floor?"

No reply, but Elizabeth caught the swift glint of Audrey's eyes. Elizabeth knew then that Cecily had thrown
the book. Callous the girls might be, but not one would
break the code by tattling. Elizabeth realized that she

had been outmaneuvered. All that was left to do was to call Cecily in and dress her down for mistreating a book. But she could hardly do that when the girl had obviously been a victim of some unpleasant prank. Retreat was all that remained. Elizabeth cast her mind about. "Oh, Audrey," she said coolly.

"Yes, Miss Marks?"

"The hairbrushes I washed this morning must be dry by now. They're on the table outside my room. There's a name tape around each. You might put them all back into their owners' cubicles."

A small, mocking smile broke over Audrey's face. "Yes, Miss Marks." She succeeded in making the request look as petty as it was. Elizabeth stepped aside deliberately, and after a second Audrey, looking better than most in the shapeless dress worn for dinner, passed her and went through the door.

Elizabeth followed and pulled the door to. Cecily was nowhere to be seen. Up in the dormitory, Elizabeth thought grimly. Being in the dormitories was against the rules, except at specified times. Yet she could hardly be blamed.

Elizabeth found her sitting on her bed in her cubicle. "You know this is against regulations, Cecily," she said mildly. "You'd better come into my sitting room. I want to talk to you."

But having got the child there, she didn't know where to begin. She glanced down at the square form in her armchair. When someone's a washout, she thought drearily, where do you start?

"You've got to pull your socks up, Cecily. You know that, don't you?"

"Yes, Miss Marks." There was a dull, resigned note in her voice that infuriated the mistress.

"You don't even *try* at anything. You go sniffling around making more fuss over yourself than anyone else. . . ." But I've said that before, Elizabeth thought, horrified. And it's not the line I meant to take at all. She was searching around, remorsefully, for an entirely new tack, when she heard Cecily give a sob.

"Everyone is so horrible," she said, and started to cry in earnest.

Elizabeth stood, appalled. She despised tears almost as much in women as in men. Only when they were being heroically repressed did she find them moving. And Cecily's sobs were getting louder. "Pull yourself together," she said sharply. "Don't be such a crybaby."

"I wasn't doing anything at all but reading," Cecily went on, still sobbing, "when they started saying beastly things, about how the air in the room was foul because I was in it and wouldn't it be nice if I weren't there at all, and then they all picked me up and shoved me out of the room." Her fingers, pushing at the tears still pouring down her ruddy face, left grimy canals.

"You shouldn't have told me that," Elizabeth said finally, fighting against her mounting contempt. What an appalling child, she thought. Had she no pride at all? She herself at the same age would have suffered almost any pain and any humiliation in total silence rather than run blubbering to a teacher. "Do you want me to go to

Audrey Leach and the others and reprimand them, making it perfectly clear, of course, that you told me about it?"

The sobbing stopped but Cecily didn't look up. Then she said in a remarkably controlled voice, "No, Miss Marks." She got to her feet. "May I go now, please?"

A little taken aback at so sudden a change, Elizabeth said, "Very well. Do you feel up to going downstairs?"

Cecily nodded, her head still down. "Yes." She added, "Thank you, Miss Marks," and left before Elizabeth could think of anything further.

That evening, by apparently common consent, she and Tim stayed away from the subject of Cecily. Worried and anxious, Elizabeth had determined to be cheerful and amusing and to keep the conversation on a light level. Evidently Tim had decided the same. In addition, he suggested they have a fairly quick dinner and go to a film. It was a spy thriller, neat, literate and absorbing, and they both emerged exhilarated. When they came out it was time for her to return to the school. Tim drove her back and parked the car under the shadow of a tree around a bend in the road and out of sight of the school itself. After a second's pause they moved towards each other. Elizabeth felt his arms go around her and gave a long sigh. "I'm sorry, Tim. About last week, I mean."

"I'm sorry too, baby," he said evenly. Elizabeth lay quiet, relishing the hard touch of his shoulder beneath her cheek. Then, before she realized it, the desire to cry, pushing from some depths within herself, became almost overwhelming. She couldn't remember even wanting to cry since she was a child, but it was on her now, in her throat and behind her eyes. She recalled the scorn she had felt that afternoon for Cecily and summoned her will power against this final defeat.

"Are you all right, darling?" She felt his arms tighten and heard the old note of tenderness. The urge to give in, to say "no," was so vivid she could feel the shape of the word in her mouth. But all her training had been against the surrender to emotion, and it was too strong. She couldn't say it.

"Yes," she whispered, "I'm all right. Just tired, I expect."

He rubbed her back a little, and she had the sense that he, too, was choosing and discarding words. "I guess we both are," he said finally.

A few minutes later he had walked her to the gate, kissed her and left.

"Everything all right?" Miss Hinsley asked the following morning as she and Elizabeth strolled back across the fields from the village church.

Her question sounded slightly less than casual and Elizabeth, for all that she appreciated the older woman's kindness, said defensively, "Oh, I think so. Why?"

"Because"—Miss Hinsley sounded firm—"I had the impression that it wasn't."

"In what way?"

Miss Hinsley sighed a little. "Don't be stiff-necked, Elizabeth. I can't tell you in what way exactly. But I sat next to your table last night at supper and it gave off an atmosphere I didn't like. After a while you sense these things. They're as strong as a smell."

"I've read where wardens say the same thing," Elizabeth replied. "You make it sound like a prison."

"In many ways it is. Any institution segregated to one sex with rules that are, however necessary, also artificial is like a prison."

"You sound like one of those labor M.P.'s," Elizabeth said, cross at herself for descending to what seemed like heckling. "Down with the public schools, and so on."

"All right. As you wish. What did you think of the sermon this morning? I thought the vicar was in rather good form."

Worsted, Elizabeth found herself stuck with a discussion of the Pauline definition of Grace, a subject that, even at best, was inclined to unravel and get totally out of hand. What was more, she had the impression that Miss Hinsley was getting a certain amount of satisfaction out of forcing her to hue to the austere lines of pure logic. Rather, she thought sulkily, like a former Latin mistress in her own school days who used to punish her by making her put particularly tough Latin unseens into lucid, graceful English. Stubbornly, she held up her end of the conversation till they got back to school. Behind it, her thoughts tossed like an uneasy sleeper. She knew very well what Miss Hinsley meant about atmosphere.

On Sunday, dinner was at noon. Along with the rest of the staff, Elizabeth sat at the high table. St. Margaret's table was just below the dais and she watched it carefully. On the surface it seemed entirely normal and just as noisy as any other house table. If not noisier. Elizabeth sat very still and listened. The voices from St. Margaret's seemed a little higher, a little more penetrating, or was it her overconscientious imagination? No, there was Audrey Leach's drawl and Biddy Elwood's somewhat affected laugh. Elizabeth, watching, saw Barbara Russell, the house prefect, frown and lean forward, obviously telling the table to be quieter. The house obeyed, but the babble rose again, touched faintly with a note of hysteria. Elizabeth knew what Miss Hinsley was talking about.

She had no opportunity, though, to watch it from any closer range until supper, when she herself sat at the end of the house table.

When a house occupied a table to itself, as it did on Sunday, the girls sat in any order they pleased. A house mistress soon learned how the friendships, sets and cliques were grouped—who was popular and who wasn't. Elizabeth ran her eye down the sides of the long table. By some unconscious tribute to seniority, the seniors usually ended up near her, then came the middle group, and at the opposite end the juniors. But Audrey Leach was sitting far down on the right side, her little coterie of four or five grouped around and opposite her. They were talking animatedly, leaning across the table. Last of all on the left side, opposite Audrey, was Cecily.

Elizabeth was busy placing slices of roast on the plates in front of her when she heard a voice—she thought it was Pamela Jenkinson's—say, "Someone please pass the bread—oh." There was a slight pause. Elizabeth, trying frantically to keep up with the plates passed down quickly by the girls on either side, glanced down the table. Pamela turned from facing the end, where the platter carrying the towering pile of bread stood, and faced Audrey. "Sorry, Audrey," she said in a formal voice that seemed utterly unnatural, "do you suppose someone can reach it?"

"Obviously, someone will have to walk around, since *no one* seems to be able to understand that she should pass the bread," Audrey said. "Oh, thanks, Sandra."

Sandra Stringer, a twelve-year-old recently up from the junior house, got up from her place, giggling, and went to the end of the table, reached across Cecily and started the bread on its upward journey. Cecily, whose head had been down, jumped and glanced around. A little murmur arose at that end of the table. "Thanks, Sandra."

"Amazing, isn't it," Audrey drawled, "how deaf and dumb some people can be to everything but what they want?"

Elizabeth's blood seemed to run still in her body. She knew the signs very well. Cecily had been sent to Coventry, the final, awful punishment a school child can visit on its peer. Elizabeth, remembering the incident of the afternoon, wondered how long it had been going on. She glanced at Barbara Russell, the head of the house, and her heart sank. That eminently worthy girl was deep in a discussion of the Higher School Certificate exams coming up in school. It could just as easily, Elizabeth thought bitterly, have been about the present state of the Anglican Church in the Marshall Islands. Barbara, the daughter of a Scottish bishop, was as inevitably destined to a life of good works as Audrey was to one of trouble. But it didn't make her a good prefect. She was studious, conscientious and blind as a bat to anything but what her mind was on at the moment. The house could plot, foment and carry out a revolution before she would look up from her book. Her predecessor would have scented trouble and put an end to it before it started. Well, if Barbara didn't do something, she herself would have to, Elizabeth thought. But it would come less well and be less effective from her.

A few plates started coming back for second helpings. Elizabeth applied herself to filling them. At Langley you did not ask for more. You waited until your neighbor asked you. If your neighbor was absent-minded, you kicked her under the table and asked pointedly if *she* would like some more.

Cecily's plate was empty. On an impulse, Elizabeth leaned forward and said to the girl sitting next to Cecily, "Laura, have you asked Cecily if she would like some more roast?"

Abruptly, as though there had been a sudden order for silence, conversation at that end of the table ceased. Now I've made it worse, Elizabeth thought. Laura James turned to Cecily. "Would you like to have some more?" she asked in a high, clear voice.

Cecily stared straight ahead. "No, thank you," she muttered.

Sunday night supper was followed by an hour in the sitting room, the only time during the week Elizabeth, as housemistress, ever sat in the girls' sitting room. On Sunday evening she read to them while they darned their stockings. The juniors sat on the floor in a ring around the fire. Almost immediately behind them, in the four armchairs, sat the prefects. The fifth and largest armchair, brought in for the occasion, was occupied by Elizabeth. The rest of the house sat on straight chairs and the two sofas in almost complete recognition of rank. Elizabeth, sitting with one of John Buchan's adventures open before her, thought of Tim's description of what he called the pecking order. And suddenly, she saw how absurd it seemed to him. But against that, as though it were a treasonous thought, spoke her instinct for order, for the peace and lack of argument surrounding everyone's tacit admission of the privileges of seniority. But it was tough on the outlaw.

Elizabeth's eyes searched the room quickly. A little back of the outside circle, by herself, Cecily straddled a straight chair, a black wool stocking draped over a darning egg in one hand, a large needle and woolen thread in the other. At the moment there was nothing to be done.

An hour later Elizabeth closed the book and prepared for the usual half hour's informal chat, fully determined to find some reason for sending Cecily out of the room and putting an end to the ganging up against her. The first part of it came off all right.

"Cecily," she said, half turning towards the girl, "we've almost finished *Greenmantle*. Would you go up and get the next in the series, *Mr. Standfast*? It's in one of the two bookcases in my room. I want to see if we can get through it by the end of term."

It was feeble enough, but it served. The book was in neither bookcase. Miss Hinsley had borrowed it to read to her own house, but it would take Cecily a while to make sure it was missing. When the solid footsteps had disappeared around the corridor and up the stairs, Elizabeth straightened herself. "I want to talk to you all about Cecily," she began.

No one spoke a word, but she could feel them stiffen as though pulled by a single string. Only Barbara Russell looked completely puzzled. "What about Cecily, Miss Marks?" she said in genuine bewilderment.

Elizabeth crushed the temptation to tell her sharply that she shouldn't have to ask such a question. "The house seems to have sent her to Coventry," she said coldly. "It's a barbarous thing to do, to anyone, for any reason whatsoever. And I want to know why it's being done."

For a few minutes there was silence. Then Audrey's magnetic voice broke it. "If Cecily hadn't made such a fuss about going into the sickroom, Ann might have been there and a doctor sent for."

Elizabeth sat there, her face stinging as though it had been slapped. Audrey was simply giving back her own words hurled at the head of the stairs when Ann was taken to the hospital. For a moment she thought of admitting her guilt and from that making a plea, and in that moment she thought of Tim. *For God's sake,* she could hear him say as clearly as though he were shouting

in her ear, *admit you were out of line, that you're human
and can make a mistake, and tell them the odds of thirty
to one against one poor kid is not my idea of the English
sportsmanship they're always yapping about.* It was so
clear she wondered if he had indeed said it recently. She
shook her head a little and took a deep breath. Then she
caught Audrey's eye, the green brilliant and mocking,
and she knew she couldn't do it.

"For one thing," she said, trying another tack, "what
about that disgraceful business yesterday? Shoving Cecily out of the sitting room—" And then she realized her
mistake. The only way she could have known was for
Cecily to have told her. The stillness in the room was
complete. Appeal to them as human beings, she told herself, and knew she couldn't. But she had to continue.
"This nonsense has got to stop," she went on, and realized as she heard her voice talk about fair play, bullying
and unfair odds that she was accomplishing nothing.

The following morning, waiting with the other housemistresses outside Miss Geoffreys's room to make her
weekly report, she found herself mentioning the matter,
with elaborate casualness, to Miss Hinsley.

"I don't like the sound of that," the older woman said.
"Have you talked to them?"

Elizabeth nodded. "Yes, last night."

"Did it do any good?"

Elizabeth paused. "I don't think so." There was a silence. Miss Hinsley said nothing. Elizabeth went on.

"I tried to get over to them how frightfully unfair it all is, but I felt as if I were talking to a wall."

"Something must be done about it," Miss Hinsley said, "And soon. It's serious. The child could break."

Because she felt suddenly afraid, Elizabeth said defensively, "These things usually blow over. You know how the girls are. They get heated up over something, good or bad, and then forget in a day or two."

The older woman looked at her. "No, not in this case. There's a potential cruelty in groups like this, a streak of savagery. And that girl, Audrey Leach, is not going to let it go, either. It's too good a chance for her to dominate. When you haven't got a strong head of the house, it's pure jam for someone like Audrey."

"And what would you suggest I do?" Elizabeth asked, trying to ignore a wave of resentment.

Miss Hinsley didn't reply for a few seconds. Then she said, "I think the first thing for you to do is to realize, yourself, the importance of doing something at once. After that, you'll have no trouble with the best means of *how* to do it. It isn't as though you hadn't always been good at handling girls."

Elizabeth felt the heat in her neck and face. "I'm not sure I know what you mean."

"Yes, I think you do. I know you don't approve of their boycott of Cecily, but I think you sympathize with the way they feel. You, too, feel she's impossible. Your own dislike is blinding you and it can do both you and her a great deal of damage, not to mention what it will do to your house."

"That is simply not true. It's most unfair—"

"Is it?" The door of the headmistress's study opened and the school matron came out, nodding to Miss Hinsley. The latter put her hand on Elizabeth's arm. "Do something soon—by tomorrow, if you can. Certainly by the week end. She mustn't go through another one like this. I'm sorry if I've hurt you, but I don't think you've been honest with yourself." She moved quickly into the study.

Elizabeth, left outside, felt as if she had been slapped. But underneath her anger and injury, like a thistle beneath the saddle, was a discomfort, an unease. She would never again feel the friendly affection towards the older woman she once had, or consider her as a friend. Yet— by next week end, Miss Hinsley had said.

Elizabeth, turning over ways and means against the braking of her own reluctance, felt a touch of panic. Then, with overwhelming relief, she remembered that the coming week end was half-term holiday. Thank God, she thought, as one reprieved. All but a few of the girls would be gone by early Saturday morning to visit family, relations or friends and wouldn't return until Sunday evening. Pupils and staff alike looked forward to it hungrily. To Elizabeth it seemed now like an island in the midst of a trackless ocean. Because it was a well-known fact of school life that the tensions and problems that boiled up with the first passing weeks had disappeared when the girls got back from their mid-term break after a day or so of overeating, undersleeping and some concentrated spoiling by their families. One of Miss Geoffreys's less expected remarks was that they seemed to return in the same relaxed stupor as sailors after shore leave.

The weight lifted off Elizabeth's shoulders. She wouldn't have to do anything. Half-term would take care of that.

5

Tim rang the following morning. A little surprised, but delighted, she told him about the holiday coming up.

"Hmm," he said, obviously pleased. "Ours isn't until the following week end, but maybe I can wangle something. If so, what do you think of going up to London, taking in a matinee and having dinner in some sleek, expensive, high-toned joint?"

"I think it sounds lovely," Elizabeth answered, absurdly glad that the gulf, or wall, or whatever it was between herself and Tim had gone. "I can leave here as soon as I get the last of my little monsters off."

"Swell. I'll call you back this evening to let you know definitely, and we can fix where to meet. This is marvelous, darling. Let's make some definite plans about the wedding."

"Yes, let's." She felt lightheaded. In less than two months they would be married, the school and its problems would be behind, successfully dealt with. Really, she thought, with patient charity, these older teachers get to exaggerate things.

Tim telephoned that evening. He had been able to trade duties with some other master. They agreed to meet in Mainbridge at eleven on Saturday and drive to London in Tim's car.

Saturday was clear and warm, with that washed, watercolor blue of an English sky in spring. By nine-thirty all the girls had gone, a few collected by parents in cars, the majority by the entire complement of local taxis, working in relays, to the station where they would catch the local train to Mainbridge and thence to London where all of them, by prearrangement, would be met.

At ten-fifteen Elizabeth, who had put on the blue dress Tim particularly liked, was slipping into her coat when her telephone rang. Tim, she thought, and wondered if anything had gone wrong.

But it wasn't Tim, it was Mrs. Matthews. Elizabeth's heart lurched as she heard the familiar, rather fluty tone. "Ah, Miss Marks," the lady gushed. "I am so glad to be able to tell you—and to ask you, of course, to tell Cecily —that we will be able to meet her after all. My husband was able to get back from Scotland, and we can meet her on the first train she can take."

"But she's already left, Mrs. Matthews." Elizabeth's mind quickly produced the picture of Cecily piling into a taxi at a quarter to nine with three or four other girls. "She said she was going to catch the nine-forty-five from Mainbridge and that you were meeting her at Euston." It was like delayed shock. Her senses and instinct had already gathered themselves for a crisis that her mind refused to accept.

"But I wrote to her last Monday that we were dreadfully sorry, but we couldn't have her with us this half term because her father and I would have to be in Edinburgh." Mrs. Matthews's voice rose ominously. "I know she received the letter because she wrote back that several girls were staying over the holiday and they'd all be together in St. Clare's. Besides," she tumbled on irrelevantly, "we've always come for her in the car. Where is she, Miss Marks? Where could she possibly go? Is she visiting some friends? But surely you would know about that. . . ."

The high-pitched voice, ignorant of all control and driven by anxiety, soared shrilly. Stunned, frightened and angry, Elizabeth tried to summon some organized line of thinking. First, she must get rid of this woman, after soothing her as much as possible, or she and her husband would descend on the school like the furies. With difficulty, and feeling as though she were pushing the woman back through the receiver, Elizabeth induced her to ring off, after repeatedly promising to call back in half an hour.

When she had hung up, Elizabeth stood still for a moment. Tim, she thought, and felt suddenly like crying. Quickly, she dialed his school number, hoping to catch him before he had left. But a breezy English masculine voice told her that Nichols had shot out of there at dawn. Poor Tim, he would have to wait and wonder until he called her to find out what had happened.

Elizabeth wrenched her mind back to Cecily, and with the thought of the child fury suffused her entire being. Cecily was like a malignant shadow over her whole life.

And then Elizabeth became afraid. What *had* happened to her?

She stared down at the phone and realized that Miss Geoffreys would have to be told. The chances were that Cecily, knowing that she was expected by the school to be gone, had decided to take an unchaperoned day off. But until handed over to her parents, she was the school's responsibility—Elizabeth's.

Miss Geoffreys, her handsome figure encased in a well-tailored, light tweed suit, was standing by the French windows of her study when Elizabeth knocked and walked in. They had had no more than routine conversation since that day (was it only a few weeks ago?) that she had walked down the corridor of the school with the headmistress and had received her first reprimand about Cecily.

"Good morning, Miss Marks," Miss Geoffreys said. "Each year I tell myself I shall become used to the sight of the first daffodils of spring. And each year they seem just as incredible. I know how Wordsworth felt."

"Yes," Elizabeth said, and drew a breath.

The headmistress turned quickly from the window. "What is it, my dear?"

The kindness in her voice was almost more than Elizabeth could take at that moment. Looking into the older woman's wise, tough, serene face, she felt a sense of shame and failure. Unhappily, stiltedly, she told her story.

When she was through she saw the headmistress's remarkable eyes on her, revealing nothing. But Elizabeth felt as though an arc light had been turned on her mind and emotions.

"What time does the through train from Mainbridge reach London?"

"Five minutes to eleven."

Miss Geoffreys glanced at the small clock on her desk. "That's only twenty minutes. The Matthews live in Surrey. They couldn't possibly meet it. It's also possible she took a train going somewhere else. Trains go through there all the time."

"But why?"

"Why did she run away?"

There was a short silence.

The headmistress went on. "She could, of course, be headed home, thinking her parents would be away and planning to leave before they returned. But I don't think so. The Matthews have servants who would be bound to tell them that she'd been there, and she'd be in trouble from them. Unless, of course, she's determined not to come back here." She glanced at Elizabeth. "What do you think?"

Elizabeth stared back, remembering the past week. "I don't know. She'd have no trouble convincing her mother, who's absurdly protective."

"But not her father, who isn't. I can't believe she'd be ready to face that bit of parental music unless she's quite desperate. Is she, Miss Marks?"

The calm, detached voice was somehow worse than an accusation. Reluctant, belated compassion touched her. "I don't know," Elizabeth said again. "She might be."

Miss Geoffreys lifted the receiver off her phone. "Please ring Colonel MacIver."

"It will be all over the village," Elizabeth said. "They always listen in at the exchange—especially, I should imagine," she added, trying to keep her voice level, "when one talks to the police."

"She could be going home," the headmistress said, as though she hadn't spoken. "She could have taken another train to take refuge with friends. Or she could still be in Mainbridge."

"Wouldn't the others have noticed if she didn't get on the London train with them?"

"Does she have any special friends who would have concerned themselves?"

"No."

"Then among all those dozens she could easily get away. Colonel MacIver," she said into the phone, "this is Miss Geoffreys. I'm sorry to disturb you, but I'm afraid I shall need your help . . ."

Elizabeth listened with growing guilt to the headmistress talking to the chief constable. The local police would have to scour Mainbridge; the metropolitan police would have to be brought in to meet the train nearing London and, if Cecily were not on it, to look for her in the city. And if she were not on the train, police from the surrounding counties would have to be alerted on the remote possibility that she had got onto another train to go to friends or simply taken off on impulse to some unknown destination for some unimaginable reason.

As the magnitude of what had happened and what

would have to be done was thrusting itself on Elizabeth, her ear caught Miss Geoffreys's voice again.

". . . Yes, of course they'll have to question the girls getting off at Euston. Even with a description it's hard sometimes to tell them apart when they're in uniform. Yes, short and rather fat, brown hair. I'm sending two of the mistresses into Mainbridge immediately in my car. They can drive around the town, and if they see her I'll let you know, of course, at once. Yes, it is unfortunate, but we must do whatever possible, whatever the cost in publicity. . . ."

And the cost would be formidable, Elizabeth thought. The girls, questioned at the station, would tell their parents, many of whom would be there to witness the hubbub. Two other mistresses—Elizabeth winced at the thought—were to be called in. Within an hour the whole school and county would know. If Cecily was not found immediately, newspapers would shout the story that one of England's leading schools had mislaid a pupil. And what some of the cheaper papers could make of it! Elizabeth, cringing, had no trouble envisioning such headlines as *Cruelty? Oppression in Posh School!* The damage to Langley could be incalculable. A school's reputation must rival that of Caesar's wife.

Elizabeth met the headmistress's eyes as the latter put down the receiver. "If Cecily had just considered . . . ," she started. Then she added slowly, "Perhaps she *was* desperate."

Miss Geoffreys cast her an unreadable look, picked up the receiver and asked for Miss Reynolds. "Miss Reyn-

olds, would you please come to my study at once, and
could you ring Miss Finch and ask her to come with you?
Yes, I know. I'm sorry about that. But this is extremely
important. I hope you'll both have time to get away
later."

So their day's gone west, too, Elizabeth thought. And
Tim would be waiting at the station, wondering what
on earth had happened, thinking, perhaps, that she cared
so little. . . . . Elizabeth swallowed hard and took a shaky
breath, and then her anguish hardened into a mounting
anger against Cecily.

There was a knock on the door. In silence Elizabeth
listened to Miss Geoffreys's brief, unemotional explanation of Cecily's unauthorized departure and her request
that they should leave immediately for Mainbridge in
her car.

"How terrible!" Miss Reynolds said.

"Shouldn't the police be informed?" Miss Finch asked,
throwing an angry look at Elizabeth.

"They have been, Miss Finch," the headmistress replied calmly.

"Well, perhaps, since Cecily is in Miss Mark's house—"

"Miss Marks will stay here until Cecily either is returned or arrives at her parents' home. And now, the
sooner the two of you are off, the sooner she will be found
if she is in Mainbridge. I suggest you ring back here
every half hour or so. Because if she turns up in the
meantime, you can go straight on from Mainbridge. By
the way, Colonel MacIver tells me there's a fair with
gypsy caravans out near Wickett's Pond. Since all such

fairs are out of bounds, I'm sure it would be the first place Cecily—or almost any child—would go to. I should look there.

"And now," Miss Geoffreys said, as the two women left, "I had better telephone Mrs. Matthews. The poor woman is excitable enough as it is. She must be frantic by now."

Listening to her talk to the obviously hysterical Mrs. Matthews, Elizabeth recognized the touch of a master. And she's a master, Elizabeth thought with awe and bitterness, because she really cares how the wretched woman is, understandably, feeling.

Eventually Miss Geoffreys put down the receiver. For the first time her face showed strain. Sitting down behind her desk, she looked across at Elizabeth. "You probably had plans of your own."

Elizabeth's eyes went to the clock. It was ten minutes to eleven. "Yes," she replied.

"I'm sorry. And now you'd better tell me if you can think of any reason why Cecily should act in this extraordinary way."

She knows, Elizabeth thought. She knows that I've failed. That I could have stopped it if I had listened to Miss Hinsley. If I had cared enough . . .

"You'd better sit down," the headmistress suggested dryly.

When Elizabeth had finished Miss Geoffreys said three things: She said, "Yes, I see. The child had no one. I wish I had known." Then she said, "I suppose it is one of the penalties of good looks and success that compassion is learned late, if at all." And then she said, "It's not really your fault. I should have known you were not ready for it."

And as Elizabeth sat there, scalded with humiliation, she realized that all three had the impartial cruelty of truth.

Tim, his hands in his pockets, strolled down Market Road towards the town square. It was the kind of day, he thought, that would make England's worst enemies forgive her her sins. And he was not one of her enemies. On the contrary. Peering through an opening between two shops, he saw a riot of daffodils in a garden beyond. Elizabeth, he thought, with her height and her fair head, was like a daffodil. He was conscious of happiness in every corner of his being. He would marry Elizabeth and take her back with him, and when they went to live in New England in the fall she would bring something of all this with her.

Stop it, he told himself, and then grinned, oblivious of the people passing. You're getting maudlin, he admonished himself, and found he didn't really care.

He was rounding the corner into the square itself when he saw Cecily, standing idly by the curbstone, watching a small flock of sheep being driven through the street opposite.

Now what the devil? Tim thought. He strolled up to her. "Hi, Cecily. Playing hooky? Whoa, there, I didn't mean to make you jump." The child looked positively frightened, and he was amazed that anyone of her solid proportions could move so agilely.

"It's a half holiday," she said quickly. She seemed to be peering around him.

"Looking for someone?" Tim asked, a bit puzzled.

"I thought perhaps Miss Marks might be here," she replied, and blushed.

"Not yet. I'm supposed to meet her later."

"Oh." She seemed relieved. "Well, good-by, Mr. Nichols. I'm afraid I must be going now." She was edging away.

What a funny kid, he thought. Something about her touched and bothered him. What, for example, was she doing by herself? However lax her parents might be, the school would surely not allow a thirteen-year-old to be wandering around alone. "Are you all by yourself?" he asked.

There was a fraction's pause. "I'm meeting my parents at the inn in an hour," she said, and blushed again.

"Well, I'm not meeting anyone till about then. How about a cup of—er—cocoa?"

Her eyes, which he had not been aware of before, he now noticed. They were a dark hazel, too green to be a true brown, and a light had suddenly sprung into them.

"Yes, thank you."

I wonder whether it's my charm or the thought of the cocoa, Tim thought, as he piloted her across the square to the Tea Shoppe. And then, I sometimes wish to God English children weren't quite so well-mannered. Prob-

ably when I get back, though, American kids will seem
unbearable. "Here we are," he said, picking a small table
near the window. "Now, do you really want cocoa or
would you prefer something else—coffee? Lemonade?
Tea? You name it."

She didn't ponder at all. "Cocoa, please."

"Fine." He beckoned to the waitress. "Anything to
eat?"

She hesitated. "Just some bread and butter."

There's been too much bread and butter in your life,
young lady, he thought. But a couple more slices wouldn't
make that much difference, and it was an excuse to talk
to her. He gave her order to the waitress and added a
cup of coffee for himself.

"Although," he added, with a comradely grin, "coffee
is definitely not Britain's major triumph."

She giggled. "That's what Daddy says. He says any
other nation in the world makes better coffee. Mother
says it's unpatriotic of him."

"Well, your coffee is no worse than our tea." Behind
the casual comment his mind revolved around the things
he wanted to know about her. Despite his statement
about her good bones, she was at present an unattractive
lump. Yet he felt drawn to her. "How's school?"

It was though she had suddenly stepped back ten feet.
Her round, guileless face closed up. "Oh, fine," she said.
And that's a lie, he thought. He had seen that look before, remembered it from his own boyhood. He tried
another and more pointed approach.

"Do you like boarding school, Cecily? Or would you rather live at home?"

"It's all right," she said finally. Her body was rigid.

He leaned forward and touched her hand. "Hey, don't look like that! You don't have to answer these questions. They're none of my business. We can talk about something else."

Abruptly, her eyes filled with tears. She stared at him through the tears, swallowing.

Appalled and embarrassed, he looked hastily around, but the nearby tables were empty. "Here." He held out his handkerchief. She mopped up her eyes and blew her nose vigorously. "Is it as bad as all that?"

She nodded.

"Why?" he asked gently.

She shook her head. "I don't know. I just seem to be different. Nothing seems to go right."

The oddball, he thought. Not her fault, not even the school. No one's, except maybe her parents' and possibly some one person who could help her and hadn't. His mind slid onto Elizabeth. He pushed the thought away.

"Do you think it might be better at another school?"

She shook her head. "No, not really."

The waitress arrived with the order. She glanced curiously at Cecily, who was struggling to bring herself back into order.

"That will be all," Tim told the woman.

Before he could stop himself, he asked Cecily, "Have you talked to Miss Marks about this? Talked generally, I mean." He felt immediately that he shouldn't have asked, that he had somehow endangered all three of them.

Cecily's face was crimson. She was staring down into her cup of cocoa. "Sort of . . . but of course she's a mistress." Clumsily she lifted the skin off her cocoa and drank some.

"Here's your bread and butter." Tim pushed the plate towards her. She picked up a piece and nibbled at it without much interest. More than her tears, her apparent sudden lack of appetite gave Tim a pang.

He leaned back and lit a cigarette.

"When I was a kid, about nine," he said, "my father was sent over to head up his company's office in France. I was in school there three years. It was tough. The French schools are more advanced than ours, and I found the French kids pretty incomprehensible. After a while I got used to it, but I kept nagging my parents to send me back to an American school. When I was twelve, they did, and I went chasing home, convinced that everything would take up where I had left off and would be all right. Well, I was wrong. I had been away too long. I didn't even talk like the others any more. The slang was different, my clothes were different, and so was I. The boys at the American school were all right. A few tried to push me around, but for the most part they just left me alone. And the harder I tried to break through the wall, the higher it seemed to be. I was miserable. The original misfit. I was too proud to tell my family, so for about two years I just suffered."

She was gazing at him with fierce concentration. "What happened?"

"Well, eventually, things did come all right. It wasn't sudden, of course. Those things never are. But it seemed that way. I woke up one morning and found myself more or less accepted."

"Oh." Her disappointment was obvious. Tim realized she had expected some magic formula.

"I know this sounds corny, like something handed to you from the pulpit or in a pep talk. But the main thing is to be yourself. And not to hate yourself. Then you won't go around pushing or, on the other hand, hiding in a corner and thinking nobody loves you." He stubbed out his cigarette. "If you just give yourself a chance, Cecily, I think you'll grow up into somebody people like." He smiled. "I like you."

She leaned forward. "Do you?" Her passionate directness was appalling and pathetic.

"Yes," he said levelly. Then with sudden perception, "And what's more, I think you'll probably be quite pretty. You have a pretty face and very nice eyes." My God, he thought, I'm beginning to sound like a bad soap opera.

The effect was cataclysmic. Her whole face was open, lit. It was like loosing a torrent, Tim realized. Given the faintest sign of approval, she was ready to fling herself at the person who offered it. A little dismayed himself, he saw what made Elizabeth recoil. Her deeply rooted reserve would find it offensive.

"Look, Cecily," he began, and then stopped, bewildered at the magnitude and complexity of what he was trying to get across. It would take years and was impossible. "Just remember what I said. Try to like yourself, and try to stop looking at other people only in terms of how much—er—affection or friendship they can offer you. Try and see them—objectively—as they are." The words were as foolish as they sounded. Faced with a task he could not finish, Tim felt he shouldn't have begun.

Cecily placed her elbows on the table. She was plainly confused but had the look of a prospector who has stumbled on the evidence of gold. She was digging in for a long session.

Tim glanced at the clock on the wall. It was five minutes to eleven. He stood up. "Come on, Cecily. I'm sorry we can't talk longer, but you have to meet your family and I have to go too."

For a second she stared in surprise. "But—" Then she flushed and closed her mouth. "Oh, yes," she said finally.

Tim smiled. "Had you forgotten all about them?"

She gave him a curious look. "As a matter of fact—" she began slowly.

Tim threw another glance at the clock. Elizabeth's train was due in at two minutes past eleven. "I'm sorry to rush you, but we'll have to finish our talk another time."

Slowly she got to her feet and followed him out the door.

"I should walk you over to the inn," Tim said, his eyes on the station opposite, "but—"

"Oh, no! Please don't bother. I'll be absolutely all right."

"Will you?" He felt that Elizabeth would want him to see the child safely in the hands of her family. On the other hand, her train would be here now in less than a minute. "O.K., kid. Run along. Thanks for joining me and have a good day."

"Good-by, Mr. Nichols. I'll try to remember what you said."

He was embarrassed at the emotion she managed to pack into that. He patted her shoulder. "Be seein' you."

As soon as she had turned the corner he ran across the square, dodging cars, and into the station. "Has the eleven-oh-two from Langley come in?" he asked a porter.

"No sir, not yet. Due in in"—he took out a large watch from his waistcoat—" thirty seconds exactly."

Tim felt his heart leap. Restlessly he strolled towards the end of the platform. They had the whole day ahead of them, he thought.

The passengers had alighted and the train was moving on when he finally grasped the fact that Elizabeth had not gotten off. He felt horribly let down, as though a balloon had burst while he was holding it. Finally he went back to the porter. "Is there another train from Langley?" he asked.

"Yes, sir, in about twenty minutes."

Tim stood there a minute. "I guess I'll wait," he muttered. He really had no choice. He lit a cigarette and started moving about again. His disappointment had now become irritation. Then reason and good nature asserted themselves. Elizabeth was not her own mistress. If any of her charges had been delayed in getting off, if anything had happened, she would simply have to miss the first train and take the next. He strolled over to the newsstand and started looking over the magazines to keep himself occupied.

The eleven-twenty-two was five minutes late. By the time it puffed in, Tim had abandoned his attempt at reading and was twisting a rolled up newspaper around and around in his hands.

When Elizabeth did not materialize, he hardly waited for the train to move before he made for the telephone booth on the platform. Somehow, despite his rationalizations, he had not really expected her on this train.

When he heard Elizabeth's voice, which sounded abrupt and tense, he forced some cheerfulness into his own. "Hey, what goes on? I thought you were going to catch the ten-forty from Langley."

"I'm sorry, Tim darling." She sounded now so tired and defeated that his irritation and nervousness retreated before concern.

"What's the matter honey?"

"Oh, Tim! Something awful. Cecily Matthews seems to have run away. She told me she was going to be met at Euston by her parents, but they rang up to announce that they were coming to pick her up in the car. Apparently they had not intended to see her today at all until Mr. Matthews got back from some trip or other. Needless to say, Mrs. M.'s hysterical, the police had to be told, and God knows what will happen. I tried to let you know, darling, but you'd already left."

"But"— Tim's mind was assembling the facts—"I just saw Cecily. In fact I treated her to a snack. She said she was going to meet her parents at the inn at eleven." But he said it with diminishing conviction. Her nervousness when she met him, her surprise when he reminded her that she had to meet her family, fell into place.

Elizabeth's voice rose. "Did you say you saw her? Where?"

"Standing in the square big as life. I asked her what she was doing and she said it was a half holiday. Then she added she was going to meet her family. But I can see now that was a hasty addition for my information. I took her off to the tea shop and fed her cocoa and talked to her for nearly an hour."

"Do you mean to say that you calmly sat there and talked to Cecily and didn't think to ring me right away? Surely you knew there must be something fishy about the child being by herself. The school would never allow it in a thousand years."

Taken aback, Tim said, "Well, it did strike me as a little strange, and I suppose I should have walked back to the inn with her, but it was about one minute to eleven then and I wanted to meet the train." Suddenly he laughed. "No wonder she was so eager I needn't bother to see her to the rendezvous."

Perhaps the laugh pushed Elizabeth over some edge. "I suppose in America you think nothing about seeing a thirteen-year-old girl, unchaperoned, roaming about by herself. But I can assure you that anyone here would know immediately that something was wrong and find out jolly quick what it was."

"Yes," Tim said, angry himself now, "I can just see the picture. First the inquisition and then the return of the prisoner. Well, I'm glad the kid ran away. I hope she has one hell of a good time to make up for the blistering she's going to get from you, that goddamned school and probably her parents, too. I don't suppose it will occur to any one of you to try and find out why."

"If you can just pull yourself together after that burst of sentimentality, perhaps you can see if you can find her before she does something else idiotic or something happens to her or—" she added with some bitterness, "—I land in more trouble than I already am in."

There was a pause. Elizabeth, responsible for Cecily, undoubtedly was in a jam. Tim said slowly, "I'll try to find her and bring her back." He was cold with anger, but common sense indicated it was the only thing he could do, for Cecily's sake as well as Elizabeth's. She would be the world's easiest prey to some smooth talker.

"No, I don't want you rolling up here with Cecily. I'll catch the next train into Mainbridge and meet you at the inn in an hour. I hope Cecily will be with you."

"I hope so too. And try and get hold of yourself before you get here." Tim slammed up the telephone.

Five minutes later, as he was standing at the square, wondering where to begin, he was a little ashamed of himself. Eagerly he found excuses for Elizabeth. By the time he had called she probably had had a couple of hours of racking worry. She was right, of course. Not even in America would a boarding school, responsible for a girl's whereabouts, allow her to go meandering off by herself. Wryly he thought of the day they had planned. Well, it shouldn't be too hard to find Cecily. Mainbridge wasn't that large, and if all went well maybe he and Elizabeth could be together by later afternoon, though there was no hope now of going to London.

But, though Mainbridge wasn't large, an hour's search around the square, in and out of the shops and through the neighboring streets produced nothing. Tim was alone in the sitting room of the inn when Elizabeth walked in. She was pale and her face looked pinched. "You didn't find her."

Tim got to his feet and moved towards her. "No, darling, but I was just thinking, it's about lunch time, and I'd bet my last dollar that Cecily wouldn't miss her lunch. If she's still in Mainbridge she's probably eating somewhere."

"Overstuffed little pig. I could shake her."

Tim hung onto his conviction that Elizabeth was overreacting from worry. "Look, Elizabeth, I know you'll be worried till you find her, but try and calm down a little."

"When I think of you, just sitting there, talking to her . . . What was she doing? Telling you how horribly persecuted she is?" Elizabeth's flame-blue eyes burned at him.

Tim's own eyes, calm, dispassionate, stared back. "Don't you feel any compassion for Cecily at all? She's not by nature the kind of kid who does this sort of thing. And considering the trouble she went to, and the trouble she knew she'd get into, don't you think she must have been pretty desperate?"

For a second Elizabeth's sense of grievance faltered before a fleeting insight into the frantic misery that must have precipitated Cecily's flight into what could only be more trouble. Miss Geoffreys and Tim had both understood it. But Elizabeth, still raw with humiliation from the same comment by the headmistress, was not ready to take it from Tim. And behind Mis Geoffreys and Tim lay Miss Hinsley's remark and her own debacle the night Ann was taken ill. Her brief sympathy for Cecily collapsed before the conviction of wrong, of failure, that had tripped her before the headmistress. Tim, touching the same nerve, goaded her to fury.

She flared at him. "Entirely through her own fault, because she's fussed and made a nuisance of herself and because she doesn't even have the guts not to be a miserable little tale-bearer, she's cordially loathed by everyone. So, airily, without giving a thought to the school, or even her wretched parents, she takes off for a day. And you seem to be near tears of sympathy."

There was a short silence, then Tim said levelly, "I think we'd better take another hasty look through the lunch places and then try the movie houses." His anger had gone. For the first time since he had met Elizabeth he was looking at her and feeling no emotion whatsoever. For four months she had touched his nerve ends and filled his mind and his senses. But his love suddenly ceased functioning as a screen. "Why don't we start this side of the square and work around?" he suggested.

She replied impatiently, "We'll each take a side and save time."

"No, we'll go together."

Without waiting for her assent he moved forward. Involuntarily he had closed himself off from every thought but finding Cecily. And he wanted to be there when she was found. After a moment's pause her long stride kept pace with his.

The fruitless search dragged into the afternoon, punctuated by telephone calls back to Miss Geoffreys to see if any of the local police had spotted Cecily. After the headmistress had learned from Elizabeth that Cecily was still in Mainbridge, and that no more trains until late afternoon were leaving for London, the London police were called off and the Matthewses informed. But the local search was intensified, and the Matthewses, Elizabeth learned, after one of her periodic telephone calls, were speeding up to the school in their car. Twice she and Tim ran into Miss Reynolds and Miss Finch, who were still cruising around, mostly in the car, occasionally on foot.

"Where *can* she be?" Elizabeth exploded once, as they circled back to the square for the fifth time. "Mainbridge is simply not that large."

"It's larger than it looks," Tim said. "The original town is small, but the rest of it is sprawled all over the place."

"We've tried the restaurants, lunchrooms, teashops and cafés—what now?"

Tim glanced at his watch. "The police have probably alerted the movie houses by now, but we might as well double check. The matinees have just about begun." Without pausing to discuss the matter he wheeled in the direction of Mainbridge's three cinemas.

"What are you going to do?" Elizabeth asked. "Have them stop the films, turn on the lights and search the place, row by row?" Her voice was still sharp with fright, but the search was being directed by Tim, not her, and there was a touch of both irritation and bewilderment in it.

"That won't be necessary. The girl in the booth would probably remember Cecily very well if she had bought a ticket."

He proved his point. "Have you," he said, bending down to address the somewhat overmade-up young woman doling out the tickets in the first theater, "seen a plump girl of about thirteen, wearing a navy blue serge coat and skirt and probably, but not definitely, a navy blue beret with the Langley emblem? Brown hair. Hazel eyes. I think you would have noticed her."

The woman shook her head. "No, sir. I would have. Particularly if she was wearing a Langley uniform. Langley girls never come here except in school parties, of course."

"Thanks a lot. If she should come, will you phone the school? There seems to have been some mistake about the time she was to meet her family."

"Yes, sir, of course." The woman favored Tim with a sweet smile, totally out of keeping with her triangular black-penciled brows and brilliant dabs of rouge.

"They certainly react to your fatal Yankee charm," Elizabeth remarked as they turned away and headed towards the second cinema. "And I must say that was a charitable explanation for Cecily's disappearance."

"Would you rather I'd have said she was lost and the school frantic? They probably know anyway, if the police have been around. But why add to the sensation?"

In silence they went to the two other theaters and repeated the performance.

"Now where?" Elizabeth's panic was rising. "I suppose she could have decamped on the first train after you bade your affectionate farewell at eleven, especially if she knew you were meeting me. Did she?"

"Yes."

"Then God knows where she may be by now."

"She's almost certainly in Mainbridge. For one thing, by then the police would have been watching the station, and I checked the trains leaving after eleven before I met you at the inn. Nothing had gone out except a local to Blundel Cross, which is smaller than Mainbridge and farther away from London. I don't go for that fleeing-to-friends theory. She seemed pretty friendless to me. The next train she might take is the five-thirteen to London, and if she hasn't been dug up before then, I guess everybody will be on hand for that." He put his hands in his pockets and gazed around the square. "She's not at the movies, she's not eating. What else would interest a somewhat depressed, rebellious girl of—"

"Good Lord, the fair!" Elizabeth suddenly burst out. "Miss Geoffreys mentioned it. She's most likely there, and she could certainly find something to eat if she wanted to."

"My God! Of course. I'd forgotten about it. Come on. Let's go. I'll get the car."

THE FAIR was south of the old town. Here remained
many of the original cottages, jealously protected by those
who resented the urbanization of the ancient market
cross of Mainbridge. Back of the cottages, where the tiny
Main River flowed through Wickett's Pond, the fair had
pitched its tents and stalls and merry-go-round.

As country fairs went it was fairly large and very noisy.
At its upper end the merry-go-round blared out familiar
waltzes. Nearby, barkers were shouting wares and ex-
horting the crowds to try their luck at hitting the bell,
throwing rings, winning a doll or a stuffed dog for the
little lady (or missus). In the meadows spreading to the
west were pens for sheep, cattle and horses, a ring where
the horses were showing their paces, and, farther out,
the contest grounds for the sheep-dog trials. Back of the
merry-go-round in a sprawl of color were the gypsy caravans and tents. The whole area was jammed. All Mainbridge and the surrounding county was enjoying the fair.

"I really do suggest we split up here," Elizabeth said,
as she and Tim hovered in doubt as to where to plunge
in. "It will take us hours to search this place."

"No, we won't. For one thing, if either one of us finds
her, it simply means taking more time to find the other."

Elizabeth glanced at Tim and was shocked. There had always been an easygoing warmth to his face that she had never questioned, simply because she had never seen him without it. Even anger hadn't touched it. Now she was gazing at a stranger with cold, indifferent eyes and a look around his mouth and chin that reminded her—most unexpectedly—of her father. To her great surprise, it evoked an unpleasant sensation. Had she, she wondered unhappily, thought that because Tim was warmer, less austere than her father, he was therefore weaker? Had that been her mistake from the beginning—to confuse rigidity with strength? She remembered Tim's comment: In England you take men at their own evaluation, and her own misunderstanding of it. Now the passing resemblance, and the reason behind it, brought pain. "Very well," she said, and found that he had already set out among the stalls.

The fair sprawled around them. Barkers selling pots and pans, chinaware and lengths of material were doing their best by their stock in trade—funny, ribald, frequently witty running commentaries.

". . . and if you're shy about admitting that you bought this at the fair," bellowed a man in a cloth cap and open waistcoat, "you can always hide it under your shawl like this. Who'd know?" With mock seriousness he slid a portly chamber pot under his waistcoat. The crowd tittered. "And let me assure you, ladies and gentlemen, that with this really seaworthy vessel, you need never fear shipwreck. . . ." The crowd roared.

Tim's face relaxed into a grin. "I wish I had a record

of this." He glanced at Elizabeth. "No, it's not genteel, is it?"

Patiently they combed the stalls, the knots of people contesting with hammer and dumbbell, the pens where animals lowed and neighed and bleated and shoved and farmers in corduroy and tweed and heavy boots talked in language unintelligible to any except other farmers. They searched the tea tent and the booths where sticky fruit drinks were disappearing down dozens of young throats. Two or three times they passed policemen walking slowly, their eyes alert. An hour later they had circled the fair once and were headed back toward the fortune-telling tents and the merry-go-round. Picking their way through the livestock, they edged past huge shire horses with their fringed hooves, their manes and tails braided with ribbons, brass ornaments hung between their eyes. The air smelt of wool, sheep dip, manure and sweat, blown through from the other end of the paddock with the odor of warm grass and spring flowers.

Tim wrinkled his nose. "Gamy, isn't it?"

Elizabeth glanced at him abstractedly. Like most English of her class she had been brought up close to the country and found it and its phenomena unremarkable. "What did you expect?" she asked with sudden humor. "Attar of roses?"

"Just a city boy," Tim murmured, stepping carefully around a fine, smoking pile of manure.

"Excellent for strawberries," Elizabeth said.

Their eyes met. Tim's face softened a little. Either could have made the one half-step. But neither did.

A few minutes later they found Cecily, standing in front of the merry-go-round, gazing dismally at the whirling horses, a large cone with some kind of dark cream foaming out of the top drooping in her hand. As they approached, some of the soft cream slid out of the bottom of the cone and dribbled down her skirt. She jumped and flung her arm away from her, only to have the remainder of the cream collapse onto her wrist.

"Well, Cecily," Elizabeth said, "it's good to know you haven't allowed yourself to starve."

Cecily's head jerked up. She stood there ludicrously, her face white above the chocolate cream ring around her mouth, the remainder of the cream dripping off her hand, her skirt sporting its obscene blemish.

The icy fury was mounting again in Elizabeth. She kept seeing Tim's face as it reminded her of her father's, and she couldn't stop the quivering spiral that was uncoiling inside her. "It's a pity you had to be in school uniform while you were enjoying your maid's day out. People generally do not associate Langley with public displays of ill-mannered greed. It's a pity, of course—"

Her face burning red, Cecily suddenly let out a scream. "I hate you! You're horrible and cruel."

Something exploded in Elizabeth. Her hand tore across Cecily's cheek and mouth. For a second they stared at each other. Of the two, Elizabeth looked the more stunned. Then, without warning, Cecily was sick, the regurgitated food pouring out of her mouth and splattering on the grass in front of her.

"Oh, my God," Tim said.

She seemed to have eaten a great deal. Various groups of people stopped talking and gazed at her. A few pointedly did not. When Cecily's overburdened stomach yielded up its final offering, her retching croaked into sobs, and she stood there heaving and hiccuping, her filthy hands over her face.

Eyes and silence seemed to surround them. Even the animals were quiet. Elizabeth started to shake and found it difficult to control her voice. "We'd better get her back."

Tim spoke harshly. "In a minute."

Apparently oblivious of the watching people, he laid a firm hand on Cecily's shoulder. "Come on, kid, let's see if we can find a quiet corner."

Having no clear idea what to do with her, he marched her past the merry-go-round to the open space behind, Elizabeth following willy-nilly.

"Now let's see." He glanced around. Cecily had stopped crying and was standing lethargically beneath the pressure of his hand on her shoulder. Her eyes were bleak with misery.

"We must get Cecily back to the school immediately," Elizabeth said. But her voice lacked conviction.

Tim's reply crackled again. "In a minute."

Three gypsy caravans were sprawled untidily in the back of the field, lavishing color, liveliness and filth, in almost equal proportions, around the countryside.

Motioning Cecily forward with his hand, Tim guided her up to the nearest caravan. A good-looking, black-haired woman clad in a torn tweed skirt and embroidered blouse was sitting on the caravan steps smoking a cigarette and watching the trio with an odd blend of curiosity, amusement and indifference.

"Really—" Elizabeth began.

Tim marched Cecily up to the woman. "Could we borrow some water?"

White teeth gleamed at him. "You intend, perhaps, to give it back?"

Tim grinned. "No."

The woman shrugged and, showing a great deal of shapely tanned leg, climbed up inside the caravan. In a few minutes she was back with a small pail and watched, leaning idly against the side of the caravan, while Tim went to work with his handkerchief. He twisted off Cecily's beret and handed it to Elizabeth.

"Here, take this."

"I think," Elizabeth said in an even voice, "we should get her back or telephone. Miss Geoffreys, to say nothing of the Matthews, are waiting."

Tim straightened. "They can wait a while longer, although I'm sure you'd much rather she'd turn up looking like—er"—he caught Cecily's watching glance—"a waif, by contrast to all those neat, clean-living, truthful and virtuous English schoolgirls."

He saw Elizabeth whiten. He bent down again and mopped with the wet half of his handkerchief at Cecily's mouth, face and hands. Then he tried with the stain on the skirt.

"I don't think it yields to water," Elizabeth said quietly.

Tim ignored her and rubbed away.

"Please, it's all right," Cecily whispered.

The gypsy woman threw away her cigarette. She looked at Cecily and jerked her head towards the caravan. "Come here," she said and climbed up again.

Cecily hesitated.

"I don't think—" Elizabeth started.

"Go on, honey," Tim said evenly.

Cecily glanced from one to the other. Her eyes lost a little of their glazed humility. She climbed up into the caravan.

Tim lit a cigarette and leaned back against the wheels, staring idly at the fringe of poplars rimming the river.

Elizabeth spoke, her voice flat. "For some reason, to-day, you remind me very much of my father."

Tim glanced at her, his eyes as gray and remote as the sky. "Why? Have I been putting you on the mantel-piece?"

She shook her head. "No, that's not the reason." Her stomach, which had been shaking, was now definitely queasy. All she could seem to recall was the feel of Cec-ily's smeared mouth beneath her hand and the shocked look in her eyes, and it was making her sick. She stared at her feet, concentrating on the dark blue toes of her shoes. If she could keep them from moving and swim-ming then she could fight off this dizziness. She wished urgently that Tim would speak to her, ask her if she were all right, using the same tone of voice that he had to Cecily. She wished— She shook herself and took a deep breath.

Cecily emerged from the caravan looking miraculously cleaned, brushed and combed. Leaping down, she stood uncertainly between Tim and Elizabeth. Tim grinned at her. "Cecily, you look wonderful." A faint color tinged her cheeks and she smiled a little. Then she glanced at Elizabeth, who opened her mouth but closed it without saying anything. The gypsy woman had taken her stance again on the steps and lit another cigarette. She was eying Tim with interest. He moved towards her. "Thank you very much," he said, and stopped. Despite the gypsy's well-known reputation for cherishing silver (and paper even more), for some reason Tim couldn't bring himself to offer cash, even though he would have liked to. "You did a very kind thing," he said.

She shrugged.

He wanted to do something. On inspiration, he put his hand in his pocket and pulled out a neat silver lighter. It was not expensive, but it looked it and had his initials on it. "Would you be kind enough to accept this?" he said formally, holding it out.

She took it, looked at it, examined the initials, tossed it lightly in the air, laughed and handed it back to him. "Good-by," she said. Tim smiled. He knew she had accepted the gesture and liked her for it. He had a sudden suspicion that if Elizabeth had not been standing there she would have taken the lighter too.

"Good-by," he replied.

Cecily turned to the woman and held out a well-shaped —and by now clean—hand. "Good-by, and thank you."

Elizabeth nodded.

The ride back was silent. Cecily sat in front between

Tim and Elizabeth, who had telephoned the school from Mainbridge that Cecily was on her way.

Tim pulled the car up a few yards from the school and parked it. He got out as Elizabeth and Cecily slid out the other side. The three of them stood in a bay-shaped area hidden by the gates.

Elizabeth said, "Cecily, I think you'd better thank Mr. Nichols for his help today." Her voice sounded alien to her. Throughout the ride a fear had been pushing at the outskirts of her consciousness. It was, of course, inconceivable that anything irrevocable had happened between her and Tim. She would, of course, be seeing him within a few days. She glanced at him and remembered that he had briefly reminded her of her father. It made no sense whatsoever. Tim's voice plunged across her thoughts. He was looking at Cecily, not her.

"Cecily doesn't have to thank me. I like her and she likes me and we both know it. Listen, honey," he went on, "don't let those—witches in there gang up on you. You've got a lot to feel good about. Now try and lose some weight and start studying. Not because I tell you, but so you can wipe their eye." He fumbled in his pockets and brought out a pencil and a small notebook. He scribbled hastily, tore off the top sheet and handed it to the child. "I'll be at Graythorne for another mouth. This will be my address in the States after that. If you're feeling low, write to me. Now run in and face the firing squad."

She stared down at the scrap of paper for a few seconds. Then she glanced swiftly up at Tim, turned on her heel and started up the drive.

Tim pulled out a cigarette and lit it. He glanced at Elizabeth, who was still standing there. "After all that, aren't you going to deliver the prisoner in person?"

She knew that she ought to follow Cecily, go in with her, but she didn't move. She wanted to say something casual and easy about their next meeting, taking it for granted, making it a fact. She tried not to remember the day, her voice, the slap. She thought briefly of Cecily, and the familiar, suffocating hatred crowded her throat. She realized that she was staring at Tim and that he was returning her gaze and knew what was going on in her mind. She knew also that he would not help her.

"Thank you for your help," she said, and turned into the drive.

Elizabeth caught up with Cecily at the front door and they went in together, silently.

Mr. and Mrs. Matthews were with Miss Geoffreys in her sitting room. Elizabeth, coming in with Cecily, noticed that each held a glass of sherry—either, Elizabeth reflected, in celebration that Cecily had been found or in an effort on Miss Geoffreys's part to calm them down and keep their attention as distracted as possible.

Mrs. Matthews caught sight of Cecily. "Cecily, darling!" Disregarding both the thin crystal and Miss Geoffreys's desk, she slammed the glass of sherry down and hurtled towards her daughter, a small cannonball of a woman in an expensive flowered hat and an equally expensive, rather tight suit. Elizabeth saw Cecily brace herself a moment before the impact, then all but disappear inside the maternal embrace. "Darling, where on earth have you been, and what do you mean by going off and frightening your father and me like this? Really, Cecily, it's too bad of you and I have a good mind not to allow you home next half term. I can't think—" In less than three sentences, her voice had passed from hysterical concern to petulant anger. But her arms were still locked around her daughter's neck.

"Yes, Cecily, where the devil have you been? Dora, leave the child alone. I want a straight answer."

When Elizabeth looked at Desmond Matthews, she received something of a shock. She had expected him to be short, thick and dimly vulgar, like his wife and daughter. But while it was easy to see from whom Cecily had inherited her strong features and her hazel eyes, the resemblance seemed to stop short of something far more important. Whereas everything about Cecily seemed to spell the word "careless"—the way she was put together, the way she thought and moved—her sire had obviously never allowed himself a disorderly thought or uneconomic gesture in his life. A man of medium height, he was as well put together and as full of latent power as a sleek bull. He was also, plainly, a self-made man: his voice bespoke the North country, and Elizabeth noticed that while his wife had obviously worked on her vowels—to their detriment—her husband had had the good sense to leave his alone. He had nothing to be either ashamed of or arrogant about: he had too much assurance to feel either.

"Well, Cecily?"

Her mother, handkerchief to face, had moved away. Cecily looked into her father's eyes. Her fear was obvious. The memory of her own childhood stirred in Elizabeth.

"I don't know," Cecily said finally.

"Come now." His voice was brisk and implacable. "You don't go through the elaborate preparations for taking a day off without knowing why."

Cecily's gaze shifted to her feet. "Well, when I learned you and Mummy couldn't come, I thought I'd—" Her glance went swiftly to Miss Geoffreys, a silent but very much felt presence by the fireplace, then to Elizabeth.

"Well?"

"I thought I'd like to be by myself for a bit."

The answer lay in the room, surrounded, at least to Elizabeth and, she thought, probably to Miss Geoffreys too, with the widening circle of its implications.

Her father raised dark, peaked brows. "Isn't this a departure? I thought you wanted to go to boarding school because you were an only child and lonely."

Cecily opened and closed her mouth as the trap of logic closed around her. Miss Geoffreys spoke for the first time since their return. "Both could easily be true, Mr. Matthews. Being an only child is lonely. But if you're used to it, the constant companionship of a lot of other people can be trying too."

"I see," he said, and he probably did, Elizabeth thought, the way he saw a problem of accounting in his vast business concerns. She doubted if he had the faintest understanding of the mind of a female child of thirteen. But then, she jibed at herself with dismal insight, look who's talking! As far as Cecily is concerned, do I? She could give Cecily's father, however, full marks for trying, which was more than she could give herself.

He lowered his head a little and looked at his daughter. "Are you happy?" he asked abruptly.

"Yes, darling." His wife, removing the handkerchief from her face, suddenly re-entered the picture. "Because if you're not happy, we'll take you straightway home with us where you'll be among people who love you." Soft arms fluttered again towards Cecily's neck.

Elizabeth felt her stomach heave. What a really appalling woman, she thought, and remembered she had thought the same of Cecily. She glanced quickly at the girl. Cecily's round face burned scarlet as she clawed vaguely at her mother's arms. "Please, Mummy!" she murmured miserably.

"Just a minute, Dora." Desmond Matthews made a superb, authoritarian gesture with his hand, and his wife stepped back like a scolded Pekinese. "I asked, are you happy?"

Cecily looked at him for a minute, then glanced down.

"Answer me, Cecily!"

"More or less," she replied in a curiously adult voice.

"Do you want to come back home?"

"No."

"Has anyone here treated you unfairly or been unkind to you?"

Elizabeth heard her own breath. She glanced at Miss Geoffreys, whose eyes rested on Cecily with calm detachment, just as though her answer could ruin not only Elizabeth but the school and the headmistress at one blow.

Cecily's face seemed to close like a small, tight seashell. "No," she said.

"Then why in hell didn't you tell someone where you were going or that you wanted to go?" His voice, so well under control while he probed for a rational explanation, now broke under what was plainly his daughter's disobedient, disorderly naughtiness.

Her own voice rising towards tears, Cecily cried, "I don't know!"

Mrs. Matthews all but shouted at her husband, "Now look what you've done, you've just upset the poor baby—"

"Just because—"

Miss Geoffreys spoke. "I think everyone is, very understandably, upset." She turned to Cecily. "Cecily, I shall want to speak to you later. You know for yourself that you've broken one of the strictest rules in the school and will have to be punished. But I want you now to return to your dormitory."

Relief slid over Cecily's face. "Yes, Miss Geoffreys." Hastily, before her mother could gather herself, she kissed her and stepped back. "Good-by, Mummy. Good-by, Daddy."

Punctiliously and efficiently, Mr. Matthews kissed his

daughter on the cheek. "You might try to do better with your marks, too," he said stiffly.

"Yes, Daddy."

Cecily turned towards the door. "Good evening, Miss Geoffreys." She gave a tentative smile. Then she turned and said without expression, "Good evening, Miss Marks."

"Good evening," Elizabeth said. She could not, as yet, bring herself to recognize, let alone accept, Cecily's gallantry. Nor did she wish to stay in the room with the Matthewses. She both wanted and dreaded to be alone. She half turned to follow. "Perhaps I'd better—"

Smoothly the headmistress interpolated, "No, Miss Marks, it might be better for you to stay in case Mr. or Mrs. Matthews wishes to ask you any questions about Cecily." Her eyes were as calm as though this were any Sunday afternoon parental visit.

"Yes, of course."

Mr. Matthews took out a cigarette and tapped it briskly against the box. "Cecily's marks are atrociously bad, and it isn't as though she were any good at anything else— tennis, for instance, or dancing. And she's not getting any thinner. Do you know what's the matter?"

Dismayed both at the magnitude and the accuracy of the question, Elizabeth opened her mouth, though she had no notion of what she was going to say. She was given a brief reprieve by Mrs. Matthews. "I've told you before, she'll lose weight when she grows older. I don't want her doing any silly dieting now. I—"

"Let me handle this, Dora."

It was quiet but effective. Mrs. Matthews's small, full lips closed.

Miss Geoffreys looked across at Elizabeth. "Would you like to discuss Mr. Matthews's question, Miss Marks?"

Through the net that seemed to be closing around her, Elizabeth could almost hear Tim's voice in garbled snatches of everything he had ever said about Cecily from the beginning. He was the only one, she thought, who could really answer. And with that her resentment flared up a little. She was aware of the man's dark eyes on her, impersonal and probing.

"I think," she started off slowly, "she needs a combination of sympathy, self-confidence and—er—stiffening. And no one seems to be able to give it to her in just the right proportions."

"I see." He frowned, probably summoning up a mental image of therapy consisting of those exact ingredients.

"Well, she has always known she could come to me for sympathy and understanding." Mrs. Matthews's voice quavered with sentiment and indignation. "As for the confidence—"

Elizabeth was tired, and the beginnings of what she knew to be a long unhappiness was soaking into her. She interrupted suddenly: "You give her too much, Mrs. Matthews. That's part of her trouble."

"Well—"

"Miss Marks is right." Mr. Matthews rapped out the words and then reached over and gave his wife's hand a short, fierce pat as her eyes filled. "You're too softhearted, Dora."

No, Elizabeth thought wonderingly, as though she were seeing Mrs. Matthews in focus for the first time, you've got your husband fooled along with everyone else. You look and act like a marshmallow, but you're about as softhearted as a barracuda. And then, because the corollary was unavoidable, she wondered how much of Cecily's irritating and—until now—senseless behavior could be traced to thirteen years of skilled emotional blackmail.

She looked up to find Miss Geoffreys's eyes on her in passionless judgment. At that moment a sense of total defeat closed in on Elizabeth. She heard Matthews's voice.

"Well, Miss Marks, as I said, what do you suggest?"

From his tone, Elizabeth knew he had twice asked the question. The words "send her to another school" were there, dancing in the forefront of her mind. She hungered to say them. But it was too late. She didn't know whether it was too late by two or three short minutes, by a day, or whether it had always been too late.

As though he had read and mocked her, he said, "Perhaps I shouldn't say this, but what about sending her to another school?"

Elizabeth looked at Miss Geoffreys, who continued to say nothing.

Mr. Matthews cleared his throat and made his first stupid remark, "Perhaps you don't feel free to say so if you do. I can see—"

He glanced towards the headmistress, who interpolated calmly, "Miss Marks not only may but knows that I expect her to express an honest opinion."

"Of course," snapped Mr. Matthews, angry at himself. "It's just that Cecily is not attractive and never will be, so she can't count on that taking her through life, and it's time she started thinking what she is going to do. She'll have plenty of money, but she'll need something to keep her occupied." Still angry, he added defiantly, "Otherwise the first la-de-dah chap that comes along and tells her she's good-looking could have her and the money, with or without marriage."

"Desmond!" his wife gasped. "What a horrible, *vulgar* thing to say about Cecily. And at her age—"

"It's true." His anger had receded but he was stubbornly refusing to withdraw.

Elizabeth closed her eyes for a moment and tried with all her might to ignore a door that was opening, despite her best efforts, in her mind. She heard Miss Geoffreys's quiet voice. "I think you underestimate—"

Elizabeth did the unthinkable: she stepped across that voice. "My—fiancé"—she started, and stopped for a second —"met Cecily. He said that she would one day be pretty. She's got good bones and coloring and nice eyes. All she needs to do is get thinner and grow up."

Mrs. Matthews's face lit up. "Desmond, I told you."

He looked surprised. "Well, there's plenty of room for improvement. But I can't see her becoming any raving beauty."

Miss Geoffreys made one of her unexpected statements. "Not for anyone who's looking for a chorus girl. But there are plenty who are not." She looked levelly at Cecily's father, and the color flowed back into his face. Elizabeth glanced swiftly at Dora Matthews; twenty years ago when she was twenty pounds lighter she probably would have been as cuddlesome as a soft blonde rabbit. Obviously her husband's taste ran in that direction.

Desmond Matthews was looking at Elizabeth intently. A sardonic light gleamed in his eye. "And you, Miss Marks. Do you agree with your fiancé? Do you think you can wake this sleeping beauty?"

Despite his blunder, he was no fool. Momentarily bested, he had gone straight for the weakest link.

Before her eyes rose the image of Cecily vomiting on the fairground, her hands and clothes smeared. Her dislike of the girl came throbbing back. It was on Cecily's account that she and Tim had quarreled; that she, Elizabeth, had behaved in a way that, if she allowed herself to think about it now, would horrify her. It would be so easy to get rid of Cecily for good: simply tell the whole story of the afternoon, leaving out nothing—not even the slap. Pride alone would force the Matthewses to remove their wretched offspring.

She opened her mouth, caught Miss Geoffreys's eye, and stopped, realizing that twenty-four hours before she never could have even contemplated such a thing.

"Well?" Eagerness to hear unexpectedly good news of his daughter tugged against Mr. Matthews's obvious desire to see Elizabeth caught in her own trap.

"I don't know," she said finally.

"Then after all your fine talk you don't think much more of Cecily's possibilities than I do."

"I think they might have shown up a great deal better if she'd had either love or confidence from you."

Dora Matthews bridled like a pullet. "Well, I'm sure my husband never means to be severe. He's terribly proud when Cecily does something well. Like the time she wrote the prize competition story and had it published in the *Girls' Annual*. He talked to everyone about it."

"Is your affection on a delivery basis?" Elizabeth asked him bluntly.

The dark red was back in his face. "I didn't come here to be lectured by a schoolmistress." He turned to Miss Geoffreys. "You're the headmistress. Can you do anything for Cecily or can't you?"

Having done her bit to back her employer into an impossible corner, Elizabeth suffered a pang of remorse.

Miss Geoffreys never looked at her. "Yes, I think we can. But I won't know positively until I have talked to both Cecily and Miss Marks about it. Perhaps I may write to you?"

Mr. Matthews paused and then nodded. "All right. That's good enough. We'll be going now."

Dora Matthews's surprisingly large hands fluttered. "And you will take good care—?"

"Yes, they'll take care of her now." He emphasized the "now." It was his revenge for having revealed himself that afternoon. "Good evening, Miss Geoffreys, Miss Marks. I shall be hearing from you in the near future."

It was not a question. Nor was it a graceful exit. It was a demand.

The room was very silent when they left. Elizabeth realized that she had been standing ever since she had arrived and that she was exhausted to the point of feeling sick. Miss Geoffreys moved unhurriedly around, collecting the crystal glasses and putting them on a silver tray at the corner of her desk. "Would you like to talk about the matter now or tomorrow?" she asked Elizabeth. "You look rather done in." Her voice was courteous but lacking in warmth. Elizabeth, who wanted more than anything to go to her room and face the pain which awaited her, said, "Now, I think, if you don't mind."

"Then you'd better sit down." Going to a cupboard, the older woman took out another glass and poured some sherry into it from a decanter. Elizabeth wanted to refuse it. There was a stinging at the back of her eyes. Sitting down, she picked up the glass and drank a little. The tightness in her body eased. Miss Geoffreys sat down in the chair behind her desk and turned it to face Elizabeth, who felt, as she looked into the magnificent aquamarine eyes opposite her, as though she were gazing at her executioner.

Slowly, and leaving out nothing, Elizabeth told the story of the afternoon.

"I see," Miss Geoffreys said. She stared down at her strong, supple hands resting on the desk. Elizabeth felt that she had been withdrawn from as though she were unclean.

The headmistress rose. "Well, Miss Marks, I shall let you know my decision." She had been dismissed.

As Elizabeth left she reflected tiredly that the decision probably referred as much to herself and her own future as to Cecily.

Returning to St. Margaret's through the school corridors, she encountered one or two of the disconsolate few who were not able to visit family or friends over the half-holiday week end. Despite their presence, the building had a desolate, deserted quality. I suppose I should go and see Cecily, Elizabeth thought as she emerged from the passageway into her own house, and hesitated. But her hand seemed to feel again the contact with the child's face, and she shrank from the thought. Moving quickly, she went straight to her room.

Closing her door, she leaned back against it. Pain came at her from every direction, seeping into her, engulfing her. Opening her eyes, she looked at her bedside clock and saw it was after six o'clock. Years ago, early this morning, she had thought all the wedding plans would have been completed, perhaps even the steamship tickets to New York ordered under the name of Mr. and Mrs. Timothy Nichols. Now—

She looked down at her engagement ring and felt an absolute certainty that all this would never take place. The pain was so intense that she took refuge in physical motion. Moving over to the dressing table she put her gloves down. A small snapshot of Tim stared up at her from a round blue-enameled frame. It was a head shot she herself had taken. He was laughing, his eyes narrowed into the sun. As the tears started a spasm of the old fury against Cecily went through her. "It's all her fault," she whispered. But as she said the words, she knew that they were not true.

7

Sunday dawned clear and bright and unusually warm. "It's not going to last," Miss Hinsley said cheerfully. "I always tell myself that so that I don't rush off in a fit of enthusiasm and put away all my winter clothes."

Elizabeth forced a smile. " 'Ne'er cast a clout till May be out,' " she quoted.

The older woman gave her a sharp look, then glanced away. "If those girls don't come we'll stamp into church in the middle of the collect and the vicar will turn around and glare. He always does. Hurry up, you two!"

The two stragglers broke into a run and joined the others waiting on the drive in front of the main door. The eight girls, relics of the week end collected from all the houses, moved automatically into a line of twos.

"All right," Miss Hinsley said. "Off you go. And keep up! I don't want the vicar making any comments about those who arrive late in the house of the Lord for our particular benefit. Or, for that matter," she added in a lower voice to Elizabeth, as they brought up the end of the line, "coming out with his favorite reference to the unwise virgins. I can't think why he does it. It always sends them into fits of giggles. . . ." Her voice rambled amiably as Elizabeth walked silently beside her.

While the others were pairing off with friends or form mates, Cecily had stared with elaborate casualness at a clump of trees. Whoever was left over would have to walk with her, and while her resilient hope had long clung to the thought that by this grab-bag method she might find a boon companion, it had never worked out that way. Depending on the girl, she was usually polite and resigned or silent and unresigned. I don't care, Cecily thought stubbornly. This time *I* won't talk. The thought pleased her so much that she snapped her teeth together inside her mouth, accidentally catching her tongue. She could feel her eyes beginning to water and glanced warily around to see if anyone had noticed. Her gaze caught Miss Marks's, who was looking at her in a strange way. Both looked away quickly. Cecily, images from the day before suddenly in her mind, felt her cheeks get hot. She wrenched her thoughts onto the more gratifying memory of Mr. Nichols. "I like you," he had said, and given her his address. And he'd stuck up for her against Miss Marks. But Cecily pulled hastily away from that memory too, because it contained the unbearable picture of herself vomiting on the ground—

"Cecily?"

Silently, and with considerable surprise, she joined the girl who was to be her companion for the mile walk to the church.

Enid Cameron of St. Clare's was the school brain. Although only fifteen she had already taken her honors matriculation and her higher school certificate and was now simply marking time until she was sixteen and could sit for her Oxford entrance. Although, according to school lights, she was something of an oddity, she was regarded with respect—not, of course, with the near adulation bestowed upon the games captain, who stood at the pinnacle of success, or the tennis captain, who was pretty, to boot. But, abject as was the adoration given them, there was also with them and about them a degree of easy familiarity. However splendid, they were still part of the pattern. Enid was not. The school liked her and was, in an oblique way, proud of her. But as Sue Parsons once said, "My God, if you know perfectly well she's sitting there thinking about the cube root of pi R squared or the origins of the human race, what on earth do you say to her?"

Now, considerably awed, Cecily promptly forgot her resolutions and said rather meekly, "Hello, Enid."

Enid smiled. She was a slight, rather ordinary-looking girl with sandy hair, greenish eyes and sharp features. She had, Cecily thought, a nice smile. Forgetting her depression, she stared at her companion with candid curiosity, until a faint color stained the other girl's face.

"Do I have a smut on my nose?" Enid asked.

Cecily flushed and shook her head. "No, sorry. I didn't mean to stare."

"Why were you?" She didn't seem upset: mildly curious, perhaps.

"Well," Cecily said frankly, "you're only fifteen and you've got honors matric. and higher school cert. and I've never met anyone who's done that."

The girl in front turned around. *"Really,* Cecily, of all the cheek—"

"It doesn't matter," Enid said quickly.

"It certainly does! Cecily, I think you should report to—"

"I said it didn't matter." Enid's voice was firm. "Now, since this is a private conversation why don't you buzz off."

Betty Whitmore, a subprefect from St. Margaret's and a friend of Audrey Leach's, hesitated, shot an arrogant look at Cecily, but turned back. Enid was smaller, younger and not even a house subprefect. But she was Enid Cameron, and for once rank stepped down.

Cecily glowed with pleasure and admiration.

"I say, Enid, thanks a lot." She added abruptly, "I'm sorry if it was cheek."

"It wasn't, really. At least, I don't think you meant it that way. Only—"

Cecily's round, worried gaze fixed on her again. "Only what?"

Enid grinned. "I sometimes feel like a freak."

Cecily absorbed the thought. "I know what you mean," she said earnestly. "Only it must be better being different because you're brainy."

Enid looked at her but didn't say anything.

"What," asked Cecily, who found small talk a waste of time, "do you like best? At school, I mean?"

"Greek, I think."

Cecily was impressed. To her languages ranked below

arithmetic and only slightly above gym in pure horror.
"Do you like gym?"

"No. I hate it."

Cecily cheered up a little. "So do I. Are you going to
do Greek when you get to Oxford?"

"No. I'm going to do physics."

"Why, if you like Greek best?"

"Because—well, I suppose that besides enjoying it
there's not much I can do with it. I don't want to teach,
and I don't see any point in putting out a fifth-rate trans-
lation of something that's already been done by somebody
else. And by comparison, physics is just beginning." She
saw Cecily's mouth open with, undoubtedly, another
question. "And what," she put in firmly, "do you want to
do when you grow up?"

Cecily knew instantly what a truthful answer would
be: she wanted to be thin and have lots of men in love
with her and marry Mr. Nichols and have Miss Marks
to the wedding. She also knew she couldn't say it, even
without Betty Whitmore, ominously quiet, in front. "Er—"
she began. And then the words popped into her mouth
without her thinking, or, to her knowledge, having
thought of them before. "I want to be a writer."

"It's amazing," Betty Whitmore said to her companion
in a clear voice, "the conceit some people seem to have
when they can't even get a decent mark. A *writer*, for
heaven's sake!" The other girl giggled.

Cecily's cheeks went bright red. It was a fatal mistake
saying that. Betty would pass it on to Audrey before the

latter had been back five minutes. Cecily knew she would
never hear the last of it. Knowing she was making bad
worse, dimly aware that she was charging into a carefully
laid trap, she opened her mouth. But Enid was there first.

"Betty," she said pleasantly, "another comment like
that and I shall stop the line and ask Miss Hinsley to take
a hand. She hates rudeness and bullying, and she'll make
you apologize publicly."

Betty turned an angry face. "I didn't know running to
teacher was in your line."

"Well, now you know. And don't start talking to me
about your idiotic code. I don't give a damn about it."

By this time there was silence up and down the line.

"What's going on?" Elizabeth muttered, startled out
of her mood.

"I'm not sure," Miss Hinsley replied happily, "but I
thought I heard a Spartacuslike warcry."

Elizabeth frowned. "Yes, but—I realize Enid's a special
case, but Betty is older and a subprefect—"

"And a vicious little bully. I'm sorry, Elizabeth, but
after thirty years I'm feeling the stirrings of revolution."
She turned to the younger woman. "And I wouldn't be
surprised but what your Cecily has done it."

"*My* Cecily!"

"Yes, yours. Oh, yes," she answered the unspoken question. "I know what happened yesterday. Or most of it.
I think she's a sort of Jacob's angel to you. And unless
you're prepared to face this and do something about it
you'll never be happy or have any peace. And you'll be
far worse off, in the end, than Cecily."

Elizabeth was battling with an impulse that she had never seriously felt before in her life: to turn and run— away from the school, the mistress and the girls. To where? Tim, she thought. As her eyes blurred she concentrated on the path in front of her, counting the stones, calculating how long it would be until she could get back and ring him up.

Cecily was trying to think of something to say to Enid, who seemed to have drifted away into thoughts of her own. She wanted to thank her, shake her by the hand, and shout. She also hoped that everyone was aware of just *whom* Enid was sticking up for. Me, Cecily thought happily. She tilted her head back a little and squinted at the sun, which seemed to smile back at her. The sense of something Mr. Nichols had said drifted through her mind. But the words wouldn't come. She decided abruptly not to say anything, then equally quickly changed her mind. "Thanks," she said.

"I'm not so sure," Enid replied. "You'll probably catch hell later on."

"Yes." She thought of the mischief Betty and Audrey could get out of her saying she wanted to be a writer, and her spirits slumped a little. But the idea itself revolved pleasantly in her mind. Years later, when she would be famous, the most famous by far of the Old Girls, and engaged to Mr. Nichols, she'd come back for the Old Girls' week end. Betty and Audrey would be there, of course, quite ugly, asking for her autograph and pretending what great friends they'd all been. . . .

"Why don't you just ignore them?"

"What? Who?" She stared at Enid for a baffled moment and then blushed. "Oh, yes. Well—" She sighed. Reality was back. "I do try, but when they start getting sarcastic I forget."

"Well, they just do it because you rise to the bait. Try looking through them. Pretend they're cockroaches or earwigs. After a while it won't be any more fun for them and they'll stop."

The idea had instant appeal. Cecily concentrated on the back of Betty Whitmore's neck and imagined her as an earwig crawling out from under the cricket pavilion. You'd simply step on her or hit her with a cricket bat. Squelch! Now Audrey. A little larger and even uglier. Neatly in two. Bang! "It's a good idea," Cecily said earnestly. "I'll work on it. Today."

One by one they all clambered over the stile and emerged into the village. The bells were going through the last of their changes. Decorously the group approached the lich gate.

"Everyone got change for the collection?" Miss Hinsley asked. "No, Beryl, a ha'penny will not do. I can't help it if you did spend your week's allowance on sweets. They're bad for your teeth, anyway. Here's sixpence. You can give it back to me at school. Pat, put your hat straight. Gloves, everyone. All right. In we go."

As Enid fumbled with her gloves, Cecily noticed her hands. Thin and supple, they would have been beautiful if it were not for the ends made stubby by bitten nails. Surprised, Cecily stared. "You bite your nails." Then, terrified that she had forfeited the friendliness of the past half hour, she blurted out, "I'm terribly sorry. I—"

"It's all right," Enid said good-naturedly. "Miss Hinsley lectures me on it at least once a week."

Somehow, the distance between them had lessened. In a burst of confidence, Cecily confided her sore point. "People are always lecturing me about eating too much."

Enid looked at her. "They probably do. Never mind. One day you'll stop." She grinned and looked less formidably intelligent. "Speaking of eating, why don't you come to tea at St. Clare's this afternoon?"

"I'd love to," Cecily said breathlessly.

"You can tell me then what you want to write about."

Exhilarated, Cecily marched into church and, as soon as she was settled in approximate comfort on a kneeler, started to work on a plot.

As the choir and clergy were filing out to the recessional hymn, Elizabeth said to Miss Hinsley, "Could you take them back without me? I have to stop in the village."

"Of course." Miss Hinsley glanced at her. "And no need to hurry back. They serve a good lunch at the inn."

Elizabeth's mind was not on food, but she let it pass with a murmured "thanks."

As soon as the final "amen" bellowed from the sacristy she was on her feet and had slipped out a side door before the rest of the congregation had assembled its scattered belongings.

She was acutely aware that she had never before telephoned to ask Tim to meet her—there had been no need to. Until recently he rang her at least once a day. If he missed her he'd keep on trying till he got her, knowing her dislike of trying to reach him at the all-male school. Now it was not just a matter of whether he were accessible but whether he would talk to her, and if he did— The speculation accentuated the migraine headache she'd waked up with, and queasiness clawed at her stomach.

She entered the public telephone booth opposite the inn, aware of, but indifferent to, the fact that she was in full view of the cars and villagers streaming from the church.

The man who answered the telephone went in search of Tim. She had, of course, to give her name, and didn't know until she heard his voice whether he would even come to the telephone. His "hello" was abrupt.

"Tim, I'm in the village. Could you get off for a while? I want—very much—to see you."

"I'm on duty, Elizabeth."

"Couldn't you get somebody to stand by for you? Just for an hour?" Feeling herself shaking, she drew in a breath. "Please."

His reluctance was almost palpable. Please God, she thought.

"All right," he said after a few seconds. "I'll meet you at the inn in about half an hour."

He had yielded, but at what cost? Elizabeth wondered as she hung up.

Thirty-five minutes later he walked into the sitting room of the inn. "We might as well go into the private bar," he said. When they were settled at a corner table he ordered, without consulting her, two whiskies. "Drink it neat," he told her when they arrived. "You look as if you need it."

Wondering whether it might not unstring her altogether, she took a gulp and felt the liquid sear her empty stomach.

Putting down his glass, Tim said, "What was it you wanted to see me about?"

She found herself examining him—the way he sat, half turned, in his chair; his hand around the glass; his face and the way his hair grew—wondering how many times, if any, she would see them again. She had loved him from the beginning, but how much, she thought now, a little dizzy from the whisky, had she taken him—and his love—for granted? She said, "I love you. And I'm afraid I've lost you. And I can't stand the thought." If I cry now, she thought, that will be the end of things. She took another swallow.

He said, "I just don't know whether things will work out. We seem to look at things differently."

"You mean yesterday."

"The difference was there before. I just didn't want to see it." He moved in his chair. "I don't think this is getting us anywhere."

"You hated it, didn't you? And hated me."

He finished his drink and held up his hand. "Two more," he said to the waiter.

"I'd better not. I didn't have any breakfast."

"Suit yourself."

"All right. Another one. It can't make things worse."

She pulled out her handkerchief. "I'm sorry. Men hate scenes."

He looked at her while the waiter brought the drinks, picked up the empty glasses, shot a curious glance at Elizabeth and moved away.

"It wasn't just slapping Cecily. It was what you said and the way you said it. Words can often do more damage than a slap. By the way, what's going to happen to her? Is she getting bounced?"

Elizabeth blew her nose. "I don't know. I don't think so. Her parents were there. They were pretty awful. Her mother all over her and her father shooting questions at her, at the head and at me. Cecily—" She took a deep breath. "You'll be pleased to know that Cecily behaved rather well. She didn't say anything about—about my hitting her. And when her father asked her if anyone had been treating her unfairly she said no."

"That was chivalrous of her. Did you like her any better for it?"

Elizabeth shook her head. "No, it showed me up. And you can imagine what it did to my sinful pride. After they'd left I told Miss Geoffreys what had happened. She's making her decision—about me as well as Cecily, I suppose. Whether she ought to go to another school." She looked up. "Tim, what do you think?"

"Hell, I don't know. I don't know anything about thirteen-year-old girls."

"No—but you like her. What if she were a boy?"

He sipped his drink, a look of wry amusement in his eyes. "That's damn near beyond imagining. She's a female creature." He put down his glass and frowned. "However—if she were a boy, I'd be inclined to have her stick it out. Leaving school like a whipped puppy won't help. If I were your Miss Geoffreys I'd hand her over to some teacher who'd encourage her, make her toe the line, which she'd do if she had enough incentive, and help her climb out of the hole."

"I could try."

"Why?"

"Well, since I've been responsible—"

He cut in harshly. "And you can't stand failure."

"Don't, Tim, please. Not now. . . ." Putting her elbows on the table, she rested her forehead in her hands. "I've spent most of the night thinking about the things you've said about patterns and the English schoolgirl and what she's been brought up to be—when I wasn't thinking about you. Maybe it's all wrong. Miss Hinsley said something like that this morning."

He stared down at his drink. "The square pegs in the square holes. Only Cecily is a round one. And there are probably others, God help them!"

"I'd like to try with Cecily. Partly because you're right. Well—perhaps mostly because of that. But—I'd like to try."

"Just don't confuse your wanting to help her with wanting to change her." He looked at his watch. "I'm sorry, but I've got to go."

"Tim—do you still love me?"

He counted out some change. "I don't know."

"Will I see you again?"

"I don't know that either."

She looked down at her hands, drew the ring off her finger and held it out.

"Keep it."

She hesitated, tempted. As long as she had his ring the tie was not completely broken. She shook her head.

He slipped the ring in his pocket and got up.

His car was outside. "I'll drive you home," he said.

"No. Thank you. I think I'll walk."

"As you wish."

She stood there, trying to force herself to turn, to leave first. He fumbled for his key, seeming, for the first time that day, off balance. "I'll call you," he said.

She nodded and walked quickly away, listening for the sound of the engine as the car turned, slowed and then took off in the opposite direction.

When she was on the path, away from the village, she let the tears come. It had been a mistake to ring him, as she had known, from the first, it would be.

Slipping through a side door near the library, Elizabeth planned to use the servants' hallway to reach the back of the main house and from there through another side door into the passageway. Sunday dinner would be over and she wanted to see Miss Geoffreys. But first she had to bathe her eyes and brush her teeth and, if possible, get a sandwich from the kitchen. The effect of the whisky had worn off, but her head was light and she knew she should eat something. But her bad luck held. Crossing the corridor to the servants' quarters, she walked into the headmistress. Aware of how she must look, of the whisky still on her breath, she lowered her head, murmured "Good afternoon, Miss Geoffreys," and was about to pass when the older woman stopped her.

"Can you spare me a moment, Miss Marks? I wanted to see you."

She had no choice. They walked in silence to the headmistress's office. Miss Geoffreys moved behind her desk. She indicated a chair. "Please sit down."

But Elizabeth continued standing, summoning herself. She had something to say and she wanted to get it out before the headmistress slammed the door by announcing her own decision. She groped for the words that she had planned on the way back from the village. But now she couldn't seem to pull them out through the spongy lightness in her head.

"Are you all right, Miss Marks?" The voice, seeming to come from a distance, held concern, if not warmth.

Elizabeth heard herself say, "I had some whisky in the village with . . ." Her tongue faltered. "My fiancé" was no longer correct. "My former fiancé" was unbearable. ". . . with Tim. I—I wanted to see him and I'm afraid I drank on an empty stomach." That's torn it, she thought hazily.

The headmistress was suddenly beside her, a hand on her arm. "Sit down, Elizabeth."

Obediently she moved back and sank, or was pushed, into an armchair. Her head was now spinning again and she put her hands up to steady it. She didn't see the headmistress's eyes rest for a moment on her naked finger, still indented from the ring.

Going to her desk, the older woman picked up her telephone. "Kitchen, please."

As though I were a drunk, Elizabeth thought, listening to the crisp order for coffee and sandwiches. The last of her self-esteem trickled away.

Miss Geoffreys put down the receiver. "I'm very sorry, my dear." This time there was compassion in her voice. It was, somehow, the final humiliation.

Elizabeth felt the sobs shudder through her. The control of a lifetime seemed to have gone.

She didn't hear the knock on the door or see the headmistress return with a tray. She was aware only of her hands being pulled from her face and something cold and wet pressed against her forehead. After a while she whispered, "I'm sorry."

The coffee was hot and, for once, strong. She still wasn't hungry and she wanted, urgently, to leave, to get away from the woman who had seen her collapse. But she made herself pick up a sandwich.

Miss Geoffreys had moved over to the window and was half turned away, looking out. "I'm sorry about Tim, Elizabeth."

She's having a perfect orgy of Christian names, Elizabeth thought. And what the hell does she know about it? "Thank you," she said.

"Perhaps it isn't final."

Elizabeth put down her cup. Finding her hand shaking, she quickly clasped it in the other. "If you don't mind, I'd rather not talk about it just now." She heard her voice, cold and stiff. "I wanted to speak to you about Cecily."

She paused, but the other woman said nothing.

Elizabeth took a breath. "I know—I'm sure you must have come to some decision. But I wanted to say before— I wanted to tell you first that I don't think it would be a good idea for Cecily to be sent right away to another school. She'd leave feeling a failure and it might carry over. If—if you would let me I'd like to work with her, give her extra coaching and so on, so that she could pull through her exams at the end of the year. If she felt someone was taking special interest, it might give her incentive to make an effort." Elizabeth hesitated and rubbed her forehead. She felt on unfamiliar territory. Words and phrases of Tim's were sliding through her mind and she found herself paraphrasing them. "If her work improved it might give her more confidence and she'd get along better with the others."

Miss Geoffreys leaned back, her hands braced against the sill behind her. The sun streamed onto her face from a side window. Elizabeth found herself thinking, If the winged victory had a head, it would look like that, and she felt the hard front of her pride shrink a little.

"Is this something you really want to do, or is it something you think you ought to do?"

After the silence had gone on for a while Elizabeth suddenly got up and stood, her hands on the mantelpiece, looking down at the neatly laid, unlit fire. "Is there something wrong with me? With the school? With the way we were all brought up? Tim talks about our being part of a pattern, square pegs in square holes, as though it were some monstrous plot aimed against Cecily. It's been going on for weeks and is a large part of the reason—" She paused. "I was wrong to yell at Cecily in front of the house, and what I did yesterday was—was dreadful. . . ." Her voice faltered and stopped.

"But right at the bottom you still think that the system or pattern as Tim calls it is right?"

She shook her head. "I don't know any more. And the whole thing is so mixed up with Tim and everything else I can't think. But I can't help wondering, if the whole thing is so wrong why haven't I known it before? Nothing like this ever came up at the schools I went to or taught at. And," she blurted out finally, "I've never behaved in this hysterical way before."

"That's part of the rub. Your *amour propre* has taken a sad mauling."

Elizabeth turned indignantly. "You mean all of this is just wounded vanity!"

"Partly. Plus a leaven of self-pity." Miss Geoffreys stared back calmly. "Don't tighten up like that, Elizabeth. For one thing, this is not the time. For another, I'm not criticizing you. What you feel at the moment is natural. You're in the position of someone who all his life has pinned his colors to the belief that two and two make four and is now faced with alarming evidence that they sometimes equal five or three and a half. It's not easy to have the philosophy of years kicked from under you."

Moving over to her desk, she shifted the chair so that

it faced Elizabeth and sat down. "Sit down, Elizabeth, I don't want to have to talk up at you."

When the younger woman was back in her chair she went on. "There's a lot of truth in what Tim said. The reason you haven't come across it before is because you're one of the rare, lucky people born in the right circumstances with the right looks and temperament for the right place and right time. You and the pattern fit each other to perfection. You've never had to struggle to conform to something alien, which is Cecily's problem, or looked at it from the outside, which is what Tim does." Miss Geoffreys sighed. "Success is not broadening. Your first piece of bad luck was running into both of them in one year so that they got mixed up with each other."

Elizabeth stared down at her hands. "And I can't bear being in the wrong, can I?"

"Nobody likes it."

Elizabeth got up again and moved restlessly around. "If it weren't for Tim—"

"—you'd be able to forget Cecily. Send her away, wipe her from your consciousness."

Elizabeth stood still. "Yes. So perhaps it wasn't bad luck—running into both at the same time." She turned. "Will you let me work with Cecily?"

Miss Geoffreys stood up, and Elizabeth was aware again of her authority. "Yes, Elizabeth, I will, if her parents and Cecily herself agree. But I want you to remember something." Her smile was tinged with irony. "It's no use giving your body to be burned, if you don't have love."

Elizabeth felt the pain throb inside her. "Yes, I know. Shall I speak to her now?"

"Yes. And then send her to me. And Elizabeth—"

If she says anything else, Elizabeth thought, turning from the door, I shall scream. I can't take any more. "Yes, Miss Geoffreys?"

"Good luck."

Half an hour later she went looking for Cecily, whom she found in the sitting room.

Plump legs crossed, Cecily was enjoying the unusual luxury of sitting in one of the armchairs normally reserved for the upper crust of prefects and subprefects. Although she appeared to be reading, she was actually also reveling in the unprecedented glory of having triumphed over Betty Whitmore. The latter, still stinging from her encounter with Enid, had started in after midday dinner when the four St. Margaret's girls had trooped back to the house.

"I suppose," Betty said, as Cecily pulled a book out of her locker, "you're preparing for your great career. I say, Pat, did you know we're harboring a future author? . . ." The words went on, punctuated by giggles from the appreciative Pat.

Feeling her ears and cheeks beginning to burn, Cecily concentrated on remembering what Enid had said. Ignore them. She chanted the words in her mind to stem the familiar surge of rage and panic. *Ignore them, ignore them, ignore them . . .*

"Are you too exalted even to answer my question, Cecily? Because if you are you can explain it all to Barbara when she gets back."

Ignore them. They just do it because you rise to the bait. She unlocked her teeth. "Sorry, Betty. I didn't hear your question."

It had gone on for about ten minutes while Cecily, turning the pages in a studied parody of reading, con-centrated on thoughts of the upcoming tea at St. Clare's, on happy recollections of Betty's rout by Enid, and on the latter's counsel, now rapidly assuming Delphic sig-nificance. And then abruptly, amazingly, the millennium blazed. Betty got bored and stopped.

Tingling with confidence, Cecily began making reso-lutions: she'd start a diary and keep it up every day; she'd have only one piece of bread and butter for tea; she'd write to Mr. Nichols, thanking him for his help and tell-ing him about her progress. He'd be impressed. He might even come to take her out or visit her before he went back to America. Miss Marks would jolly well know that—

"Cecily, may I speak to you a minute?"

Cecily jumped and stared, feeling some of her confi-dence ooze away. Talk of the devil and he appeared. Miss Marks waited in the doorway.

Now what, Cecily thought, as she tramped up the stairs behind the young mistress. Once again a sense of panic hovered in the wings. She glanced swiftly at the oaken door of the sickroom at the end of the corridor and her own image sprang there, a balloon swathed in a blue dressing gown, with heads staring at her, hanging from above over the stair well and along the halls, and a voice coming at her like a whip from where Miss Marks stood, her fair head shining under the hall light.

"Come in, Cecily. Sit down."

With fear a dull lump in her stomach, Cecily sat on the edge of the sofa. Her mind took the bit and galloped: I want to leave, right away. Daddy said I could. Suddenly she was quite sure that Miss Marks was going to tell her she was to be expelled. Paradoxically, it was no relief. A sense of disgrace washed over her, and she could see her father's eyes looking at her with disgust and disappointment.

To Elizabeth, the scene was an ironic parody of the one she'd just left, with herself in the directing role, offering the amenities. Gathering her resolution, she sat down opposite Cecily. With the afternoon light against her face, Cecily's hazel eyes were a tawny green and propped wide with obvious apprehension.

And no wonder, Elizabeth thought. "I wanted to apologize to you, Cecily, for slapping you yesterday." She saw the eyes quiver and plowed on. "And for the way I talked to you. It was extremely naughty of you to run away and to worry us all like that, and very unfair to your parents. But"—she tightened her clasped hands—"I shouldn't have said some of the things I did. I'm very sorry. I hope you will try and forget about them and—forgive me." Pride pushed her to hurry on, but curiosity was stronger. What would the child say? She found herself looking at her, as though for the first time.

Astonishment, relief, discomfort, and some of the old

hero worship came together. "It's—I—" Cecily cleared her throat. Nervously she started pleating her skirt. "It's all right," she mumbled. "I mean, I know I shouldn't have gone like that. . . ." Embarrassment flooded her and she lowered her eyes. But you still don't like me, she thought. You still think I'm a fat pig. She felt the treacherous sting of tears and blinked rapidly.

Oh, God, Elizabeth thought, she's going to cry. Well—Tim's voice seemed to come from somewhere above and behind her—and what were you doing this morning? "If you want to cry, Cecily, it's all right. And I won't say anything beastly." Astonished at herself, she added, "I've been doing some myself."

Cecily pulled a large and predictably dirty handkerchief out and blew her nose. Above it she stared at Elizabeth. "I can't imagine you ever crying."

"Why? Because I'm grown up?"

Cecily gave her nose a final scrub and removed the handkerchief. Exerting her imagination she tried to imagine the patrician head lowered, eyes welling, the clear voice choked. The image evoked satisfaction and a pleasurable tenderness. Embarrassed again, she looked down. "No, Mummy cries heaps of times. It's just—" she struggled with an unwieldly thought.

"I think I understand," Elizabeth said dryly. "But I think you don't realize that other people aren't as unlike you as you think they are." The faint beginnings of an understanding of the odd creature opposite her stirred. "They're not godlike, and you're not a worm."

They stared at each other in mutual surprise, and for

a few seconds there was silence while they worried at their own preoccupations.

"There's something else," Elizabeth said finally. She outlined her plan. "You're pretty far behind, Cecily. But if I helped you all I could, and if you really worked—it would mean no more half holidays and you'd have to do extra prep over the week ends—you might be able to pass the exams at the end of the year. Do you think you could manage it?"

Cecily nodded vigorously. "Oh, yes. I *know* I could. With you helping me, I mean." Already she could see herself at her desk, or up here in the study, working methodically, conscientiously, Miss Marks bending over her, paying heaps more attention to her than to anyone else, the compliments from the other mistresses—"Cecily, you've really done very well on this test, the rest of you might take Cecily's example and show what you can *really* do"; Miss Marks's growing admiration and friendship—"Cecily, I had no idea you could write so well, you really must do something with it"; her father beaming—"Miss Geoffreys seems to want you back pretty badly next year"; the friendship with Miss Marks that would go on forever. . . .

"Cecily!"

Cecily jumped.

"That's the third time I've spoken to you. What on earth are you doing?" Miss Marks sounded suddenly like her old self.

Cecily felt her cheeks burn. "Sorry, Miss Marks."

"You know you haven't a hope of pulling this off if

you're going to go wool-gathering." She stared curiously at her. "What were you thinking about?"

Cecily stared back. The lovely pictures had vanished. "I'm afraid I was daydreaming, Miss Marks. I often do."

Elizabeth opened her mouth and then closed it. She felt tired and drained. It would be so easy to snap, pushing things back into their right order. What a time to daydream! And who but this child would have said that? A weary smile touched her mouth. "I think you're a genuine eccentric, Cecily." She noticed Cecily brighten. "But don't get conceited about it. You're still going to have to work extremely hard and not just in spurts of enthusiasm. You're bright, and if you just use that imagination of yours constructively I think you can do it. But nobody except you can put all that you have to have inside your head. Now will you try—and keep on trying?"

Cecily nodded. Her eyes were bright and she kept a controlling grip on the pictures, which were coming back. "Yes, Miss Marks, I'll try. I promise."

"All right. That's settled then. We'll start tomorrow. If your family agrees." She stood up and Cecily got hastily to her feet. Elizabeth looked down at her. "Do you think they will agree—your family, I mean?"

Cecily nodded. "Oh, yes. Daddy's always wanted me to do well. And he doesn't like things not to work."

"Well, we'll try not to disappoint him," Elizabeth said dryly. "By the way, Miss Geoffreys would like to see you. Run along there now and I'll ring her and tell her you're on your way."

*   *   *

"Sit down, Cecily."

The large armchair engulfed her and her toes missed the floor by an inch. Miss Geoffreys grasped the problem at once. "Why don't you sit back? You can use this footstool." Ensconced against the back of the chair with her feet resting on the footstool that the headmistress had thoughtfully produced, Cecily crossed her ankles and stared back at the older woman in the chair opposite and wondered a little nervously what was about to come. A lecture, almost certainly.

"You've had a rather bad time of it, haven't you, Cecily?"

Cecily was astonished, but something in the headmistress's face, or perhaps voice, stopped the soft, familiar thrust of self-pity. Her eyes grew rounder. "It's been difficult," she said solemnly.

Miss Geoffreys smiled. Seeing her, Cecily flushed, looked angry and lowered her head.

"You're an only child, aren't you?"

"Yes."

"Yes, well, when one is an only child and one's parents are as devoted as yours are to you—oh, yes, they are," she interpolated, as Cecily suddenly glanced up— "I know your father is impatient, sometimes, but that's just his way of showing how much he cares. People have different ways of showing love, you know—as I was saying, when you've been brought up alone and never been away before it's sometimes hard to get things in proportion." She looked into Cecily's questioning gaze. "Do you understand what I mean?"

Cecily stared back into the brilliant eyes. "You mean I make too much fuss about things?"

"I think you're so busy feeling something yourself, you don't leave much time for wondering how other people feel."

Cecily clasped her hands across her middle. "Miss Marks said I made more fuss than all the others in the house together."

Miss Geoffreys's brows came together. "Perhaps you do. Perhaps also it's not your fault. That's what I mean by not having had to consider other people. But I think it's time you tried."

"I do try," Cecily was saying, "but—"

There was a knock on the door and a maid poked her head in. "Mr. Matthews to see you."

Cecily's mouth opened. Miss Geoffreys glanced at her and then back at the maid. "Is he in the sitting room, Megan? Good, then ask him to wait a few minutes, please."

"He's come to take me away," Cecily said woefully.

"Do you want to leave, Cecily?"

She shook her head. "No. Not now. Miss Marks said she would help me with work so that I can get through the exams. And besides—" She paused.

"Well?"

"Enid Cameron's asked me to tea this afternoon at St. Clare's."

The headmistress sorted this out. "You mean things have been picking up?"

"Yes, and—"

"And what?"

"Well, when B—er—someone was teasing me today, I remembered something Enid had said and"—she blushed —"someone else, and didn't answer back. I mean, I pretended not to notice."

Miss Geoffreys regarded her thoughtfully, searching for the right thing to say. Apparently a number of people had been saying things. Cecily's face, ludicrously transparent, was somehow registering both smugness and fear. "I'm glad you want to stay and that you've made up your mind to work." She added with gentle emphasis, "It won't be easy, you know. The things that have made you unhappy will still be there—they're not going to change all of a sudden. People will still tease you. You'll get discouraged and want to slump."

Cecily eyed her. "I suppose," she said, "that's when I'll have to remember most."

"Yes, it is. If things get too bad you can come and see me—or talk to Miss Marks. But we can't do it for you. You'll have to do it yourself."

"Miss Marks said that."

Miss Geoffreys rose. "I'm going now to get your father and bring him in here so that you can talk to him alone."

Fear came back to Cecily's face. She struggled hastily to her feet. The headmistress looked down at her. "We haven't talked about your punishment for running away, have we?"

"No, Miss Geoffreys."

On an impulse the headmistress said, "What do you think would be fair, Cecily?"

Cecily eyed her. "Well—no half holidays, I suppose, till the end of term, and extra work—except that I'm going to have to work through the half holidays anyway."

"Yes, you are. If you do what you say you're going to do, Cecily, we'll call it square. All right?"

"Yes, all right, Miss Geoffreys."

Desmond Matthews eyed his daughter, feet planted firmly on the headmistress's hearthrug, hands behind her back. She looked, to his eye, neither humble nor resigned, nor even remotely aware of the uproar she had caused. She looked, if anything, mulish, and the worried affection with which he had made the return trip to school retreated before a rising, familiar irritation. He forgot the precautionary statements the headmistress had made back in the sitting room. "Well, Cec, you seem to have made a sad mess of things."

Cecily, who had planned to be calm, was also suffering familiar emotions. "You always say that. You never give me a chance to say anything."

He spoke heavily. "Now, now. There's no need to get in such a heat. But after all the fuss you made about coming to this school, and all the money it's costing, you don't seem to be doing any work and then you run away, worrying your mother and me half stiff and making us all ashamed of you."

Cecily's face went a deep red and the tears welled and broke. Burrowing the heels of her hands into her eyes, she started to sob.

Too late, the headmistress's words came back to him:

Don't expect too much, and please, Mr. Matthews—try
not to be too harsh with her. She's absurdly vulnerable.

He remembered also that he'd intended to kiss her
when he came in, give her a pat or two on the back by
way of encouragement. But then he'd expected a crest-
fallen child, grateful for his forgiveness. It was the stubborn, cocky look that did it, as though she'd done something to be pleased about. Angry with himself and with
her, he rapped out, "Stop that, Cecily. If you don't I
shall send for your things and take you home." The sobs
died to hiccups. "Nine years," he went on, "I was in
grammar school, and nothing like this. And the last two
years working at night in the foundry. I send you to one
of the top schools in the country and you throw it away."

Cecily rubbed her eyes, then stared at her father's
stocky form and square features. She saw her own eyes
staring back at her and hated them. The image of Timothy Nichols drifted across her mind and smiled at her,
but it lacked the reality of her parent, the prototype of
herself, standing before her. Other images came, saved
up from Speech Day and parents' visits: tall men smiling
down at their adoring progeny who hurtled at them with
delight, laughing, walking hand in hand across the school
lawn, the gentle teasing about marks, but not as though
they were important.

She took a breath. "Other fathers talk and make jokes
and act as though they liked their daughters. I know;
I've seen them here. But you never do. You never talk
to me about anything except what I do wrong."

"Now look here—"

Cecily continued desperately, "It's true. I've never said it before. I've always been afraid. But it's true."

They stared at each other. He could look at a blueprint and see in the last detail of stone and timber, iron and steel, the creation it predicted. He could not look back over thirteen years and see a pattern. What came to him were his own images: small, fair, delicately made little girls, well mannered and well bred, invited home to tea with Cecily—"Yes, Mr. Matthews, no, Mr. Matthews," quiet, waiting decorously till they were offered a sandwich or piece of cake or a second helping. And instead of such a daughter, he had Cecily, noisy, showing off till he wanted to shout at her and often did.

He put his hands in his pockets, allowing the words Cecily had just said to come back to him slowly, so that he wouldn't lose his temper. How untidy she was, he thought testily, with her flyaway brown hair either too long or too short, he couldn't decide which, her blouse half out and her stockings wrinkled. Finally, as her words sank in, pain uncoiled in him, and tenderness and a baffled guilt. He cleared his throat. "You've no call to say that, Cecily. I try to talk to you, more often than you think. But you cry and fly off the handle and run to your mother complaining that I've hurt you when I don't know what I've said."

Words of denial were bubbling up, but something in her father's face stopped them. Instances, shorn of exaggeration and the rearrangement of hindsight, rolled through her mind. She said nothing, but her father caught the halting and change of expression.

"The headmistress says you want to stay. Is that right?"

"Yes, Daddy. I'll try to work. Really I will."

"Well—" He took his hands out of his pockets and nervously buttoned his jacket. "Do your best." He moved forward and awkwardly patted her cheek. "Make your old Dad proud of you."

She scowled and jerked her head.

He tried to right his error. "I am, anyway, Cec."

"You only say so when I get good marks."

"Well, that's what life's for—to do something with," he said in exasperation. "But I am proud of you, all the time. And if you don't know it, you ought. Now say good-by to me. Your mother will be worried if I'm not back soon."

She stretched up and kissed him on the cheek. He closed his arms around her in a quick, tight hug. "I love you," he said scoldingly. "You ought to know that, too." She kissed him again.

"Now," he said, untangling himself, "try for goodness sake not to get so worked up over things. Life's a long time."

Upstairs in St. Margaret's Elizabeth sat at her desk staring at nothing. In front and beside her the sun slanted through the trees into the windows. Beyond lay the downs, serene and remote, and back of them, out of sight, lay the sea. It will be fine tomorrow, she thought, but no pleasure came with it. With a sigh she pulled the top notebook off a pile near the telephone. May as well get through the third form's compositions before the onslaught of returning girls. But her eyes stayed on the telephone. "I'll call you," Tim had said. And since he said so, he would. But whether it would be only to say good-by she wouldn't know until he did. And until then all she could do would be to wait. Wearily she pondered the course of pushing him from her mind, resolving that the matter was finished, over, done with, dead. "You can do anything, once you've made up your mind," her father used to say, and for most of her life she had marched stalwartly forward, confident that he was right. But not now. That was one self-deception gone. As in the legend, you could pull everything out of the box and at the bottom would remain hope, stubbornly alive. And she wanted it alive, with all its pain. Better the quick than the dead. She would wait.

Pulling her eyes from the telephone she opened the notebook and with her red pencil started inserting inflamed-looking commas, semicolons and full stops in a sentence that meandered for ten lines, innocent of punctuation and regardless of verb, clause and participle.

Holland, Isabelle
Cecily

Old Charles Town Library

RULES

1. Books may be kept two weeks and may be renewed once for the same period, except 7 day books. A fine of five cents a day will be charged for overdue 7 day books.

2. A fine of 3 cents a day will be charged on each book which is not returned according to the above rule. No book will be issued to any person incurring such a fine until it has been paid.

3. All injuries to books beyond reasonable wear and all losses shall be made good to the satisfaction of the Librarian.

4. Each borrower is held responsible for all books drawn on his card and for all fines accruing on the same.

DEMCO